He closed the last inch between them and their lips met.

The kiss was exquisite. Not cherries or strawberries. They were both too sweet. Blackcurrant, perhaps. Tart and as complex as wine.

How long had he been dreaming of taking her, right here on the white velvet divan? His fantasies had been innocent compared to this. He had not imagined this helpless feeling of abandon as her body touched his. She fitted perfectly against him, the curve of her hip in his hand. He ran his hand over the bare skin of her shoulder, circling to the back of her neck so that he might press her mouth to his. Such a delicate nape, fringed with the soft hair he had longed to stroke. He rubbed it with his knuckle and her lips opened, eager for him.

One kiss and she was driving him mad. He wanted to ravish her with his mouth, claim her body as his own.

If he felt so about an innocent touch, how would he survive a more intimate one?

AUTHOR NOTE

I often come up with interesting titbits of information when writing my stories. *A Ring from a Marquess*, with its Bath setting and its female shop owner, was brimming with details—some of which I couldn't use.

Unfortunately Thomas Loggan, who died in 1788, was too early for this story. Thomas was appointed 'Dwarf to the Prince and Princess of Wales'—a curious title, but not his most interesting claim to fame. He was also a designer and painter of fans, doing much of his work in Bath, and often painting himself into the pictures that decorated his work.

An even earlier story that I could not use was of the hazards of communal bathing in the famous Bath waters. In 1734 you would not have wanted to share with the Duchess of Norfolk. She was a rather large woman, and her desire that the bath be filled to her chin put the smaller ladies around her at risk of drowning.

And now I hope you enjoy *A Ring from a Marquess*. And if you happen to be reading in the tub keep your chin up...

A RING
FROM A MARQUESS

Christine Merrill

First published in Great Britain 2015
by Mills & Boon, an imprint of Harlequin (UK) Limited,
Large Print edition 2015
Harlequin (UK) Limited, Eton House, 18-24 Paradise Road,
Richmond, Surrey TW9 1SR

© 2015 Christine Merrill

ISBN: 978-0-263-25557-7

Harlequin (UK) Limited's policy is to use papers that are natural,
renewable and recyclable products and made from wood grown in
sustainable forests. The logging and manufacturing processes conform
to the legal environmental regulations of the country of origin.

Printed and bound in Great Britain
by CPI Antony Rowe, Chippenham, Wiltshire

Christine Merrill lives on a farm in Wisconsin, USA, with her husband, two sons, and too many pets—all of whom would like her to get off of the computer so they can check their e-mail. She has worked by turns in theatre costuming and as a librarian. Writing historical romance combines her love of good stories and fancy dress with her ability to stare out of the window and make stuff up.

Visit the author profile page at millsandboon.co.uk for more titles

To Melanie Hilton,
for some fabulous information about Bath.

Bowing,
as always, to your superior knowledge.

Chapter One

Margot de Bryun ran a professional eye over the private salon that had once been the back room of Montague and de Bryun Fine Jewellery, then paused to plump the velvet pillows on the *chaise*. The old shop had been a rather stuffy place. But now that she was in charge and the late and unlamented Mr Montague's name had been scrubbed from the gilt on the windows, she felt that the design was cheerfully elegant. The walls were white and the columns on either side of the door were mirrored. In the main room, the gold and gems lay on fields of white velvet and carefully ruched blue silk, in cases of the cleanest, clearest glass.

Once she was sure the stock was in order, she checked each shop clerk to make sure their uniforms were spotless. The female employees wore pale-blue gowns and the gentlemen a not-too-sombre midnight blue. She inspected them each morning, to be sure that no bow was crooked, no button unpolished, and no pin in a pinafore out of line. She required nothing less than perfection.

She took great care with her own appearance as well, making sure that it did not distract from the wares on display. It was vain of her to dote on it, but she shared her sister's fine looks. Until her recent marriage, Justine's beauty had brought her nothing but misery and Margot wanted no share of that. Better to dress simply than to attract the attention of alleged gentlemen who thought a slip on the shoulder would be preferable to an honest living in trade.

But neither did she want to appear dowdy. She avoided bright gowns and excessive jewellery in favour of the same simplicity that decorated the shop. Today's gown was a muslin as white as the walls with a gold ribbon at the waist to match the amber cross worn on a thin gold chain around her neck.

Such aloof elegance inspired awe from the customers and not the discomfort gentlemen sometimes felt in surroundings they deemed overly feminine. They left de Bryun's Fine Jewellery convinced that they had gone no further than the anteroom of the female realm to seek advice on those strange creatures from an oracle. They trusted that the luminous Miss de Bryun would know better than any other jeweller in Bath what their wives, daughters, and even their ladybirds might want in way of a gift. And it amused Margot to be treated as a high priestess of human ornament.

It was good for business as well. When she had taken over the shop she had not been able to make head or tail of the books that Mr Montague had kept. She suspected that the profits had been meagre. The majority of them must have gone into his own pockets, for she and Justine had gained little more than modest allowances when he had been in charge.

But now that the business was totally in control of the de Bryun sisters, the figures in the ledger showed a careful line of sales adding to a tidy profit. Her sister, who had sworn that there were nothing but bad memories in it for her, could not help but smile at the success Margot had made of their father's business. Justine might not need the fat cheque Margot sent her each quarter, but it was concrete proof that her little sister was more than capable of handing the place on her own,

Once she was sure all was in order, Margot gave a nod of approval to the head clerk, Jasper, who unlocked the door and turned the sign in the window to indicate they were open for business. Only a few minutes passed before the brass bell on the door jingled and one of her best customers crossed the threshold.

And, as it always did when the Marquess of Fanworth entered her shop, Margot's breath caught in her throat. He was probably going to make another purchase for one of his many mistresses. There must be several Cyprians fawning over him. What single woman could wear as much jewellery as he seemed to buy? Since arriving in Bath, he'd visited her shop at least once a week. Sometimes, it was twice or more.

When such a smart gentleman took a liking to her humble business, it brought other patrons with equally full pockets. That was the main reason she took such care to treat him well and stay in his favour. He was good for business.

Or so she told herself.

Who could blame her heart for fluttering, at least a little, upon his arrival? Lord Fanworth was a most handsome man. In her opinion, he was the handsomest man in Bath, perhaps in all of England. His chestnut hair gleamed in the morning sunlight, even as his broad shoulders blocked the beams that came to her from the open door.

But it was so much more than his looks or his patronage that made him her favourite customer. He did not buy a *bijou* and hurry away. He lingered over each transaction, sipping wine and chatting with her in the private salon reserved for her most important customers.

When they talked, it was as if there was no difference in their ranks. To speak with him made her feel as important as one of the great ladies who sometimes frequented the shop, dithering over the baubles in the glass cases that lined the walls of the main room. In truth, she felt even more important than that. They might speak briefly with Lord Fanworth in the crush of the pump room or the assembly rooms. But each time he visited de Bryun's she had his full attention for an hour, or sometimes more. He treated her like a friend. And she had far too few of those.

Today, his emerald-green eyes lit when they fell upon her, standing behind the main counter. 'Margot,' he greeted her with a bow and a broad smile. 'You are looking lovely this morning, as always.'

'Thank you, Mr Standish.' That was how he had introduced himself, on the first day he had come to her. Not with a title, but with his surname, as though he was an ordinary man. Did he truly think his noble birth was so easy to disguise? Everyone in town knew of him, whispered about him and pointed behind their fans as he walked down the street.

But if he wished to be anonymous, who was she to enquire his reason? Nor would she demand formality from him. Her heart beat all the harder whenever he said her Christian name. He pronounced it with the softest of Gs, ending in a sigh. It made him sound like a Frenchman. Or a lover.

That thought made it difficult to look him in the eye. She dropped her gaze as she curtsied, to compose herself before returning his smile. 'What may I help you with today?'

'Nothing important. I have come to find a trinket.' He pinched his fingers together to indicate how insignificant it was likely to be. 'For my cousin.'

In her experience, the smaller he made the purchase sound, the more money he was about to spend. 'Another cousin, Mr Standish?' she said with a sly smile. 'And I assume, as always, it is a female cousin?'

He sighed theatrically. 'The b-burdens of a large family, Margot.'

After one such visit, she had taken the time to check Debrett's and discovered that his family was exceptionally tiny and, other than his mother and one sister, exclusively male. 'Such a large family and so many of them undecorated females,' she said playfully. 'Do you not have a single piece of family jewellery to offer them?'

'Not a stone,' he said with a solemn shake of his head.

She gestured towards the door that led to the salon. 'Well, we must help you with this immediately. Come. Sit. Take a glass of wine with me. We have something to suit, I am sure.' She touched the arm of the nearest shop girl and whispered the selections she wished brought from the safe and the show-cases. The work she had just finished for him must be delivered as well. She had been waiting all week to see his reaction to it.

Then she held aside the gauzy white curtain that separated the private salon from the rest of the shop so that he might enter. There was already a decanter of claret waiting on a low table beside the white-velvet divan.

As she passed the doorway to the workroom, she caught a glimpse of Mr Pratchet shifting nervously in his seat at the workbench. He did not like the special attention she paid to the marquess. She frowned at him. What Mr Pratchet liked or did not like was of no concern. She had hired him as a goldsmith, but he sometimes got above himself in thinking that he was a partner here and not just another of Margot's employees. To take orders from a woman, and a young woman at that, must be quite difficult for him.

But he would have to learn to do so, she thought,

with a grim smile to herself. If he harboured illusions that his talent with metals made him indispensable, he was quite wrong. Nor did she intend to marry him so that control of the shop might fall to him. Mr Pratchet was the third man to occupy the workbench since she had taken over the business. The last two had found themselves without a position at the first suggestion that their place at de Bryun's would be anything more than backroom craftsman.

Before she could step through the curtain to follow the marquess, Pratchet came to the doorway and whispered, 'It is not wise for you to be alone with a gentleman in a private room. People will surely talk.'

'If they did not speak of what went on here, when Mr Montague was alive, I doubt they will have anything to say about me,' Margot said firmly. The whole town had turned a blind eye to Montague's mistreatment of Justine, ignoring the fact that she was more a prisoner than an owner of half the shop. No one had offered to help her. Nor had Montague's unsavoury behaviour halted custom. Why should her innocent interaction with a member of the nobility be a cause for talk?

'Lord Fanworth is a perfect gentleman,' she added, glancing wistfully towards the salon. Almost too perfect, if she was to be honest.

'He is a rake,' Mr Pratchet corrected. 'A gentleman would not lie about his identity.'

'Who are we to question the ways of the gentry?' she said with a smile. 'If he wishes anonymity when visiting my humble stop, then I am the last person who will deny it. Especially not while he is such an excellent customer. And since the curtain that separates us from the main room is practically transparent, I am hardly secluded with him.' She passed a hand behind the cotton to demonstrate. It had been a particularly clever addition of hers, she was sure. It gave privacy to the more important clients, while giving the less important ones a glimpse into the dealings of the *ton*-weary aristocrats. If they should happen to gossip that Lord Fanworth had been seen at de Bryun's today, there would be all the more customers tomorrow, hoping to catch a glimpse of him.

But there would be no customers at all if her

employees scolded her instead of working. 'Please tend to your job, Mr Pratchet. There is a necklace with a clasp that needs mending and I wish to see the setting for my most recent design by this afternoon at the latest. You had best hurry for you have not even carved the wax for it.'

Pratchet looked as if he wished to correct her, then thought the better of it and went back to his station without another word.

Only then did Margot sweep through the curtain, letting it whisper shut behind her. Before approaching the marquess, she resisted the urge to check her appearance in one of the many mirrors on the shop walls. But a single glimpse wouldn't hurt. It was only to be sure that she was showing the proper, professional smile that such a good customer deserved.

And a professional relationship was all this was. Mr Pratchet was right in part. Lord Fanworth was a rake and a very handsome one. For the sake of her reputation, she'd never have dared speak to him outside of de Bryun's.

But Mr Standish made her smile. And it was no polite, ladylike raise of the lips. It was far too close to a grin. When he realised that he could make her laugh, he went out of his way to do so. His visits were the highlight of her day.

But it was more than that, she was sure. He acted as if it was also the best part of his day to sit in the salon with her, drinking wine and spending his money. Today, his features lit into a dazzling smile at the sight of her. Then, he leaned forward, eager for her company.

Without his asking, she poured the wine into a crystal glass and offered it to him, pulling up a cushioned stool to sit beside him, as he drank. 'And what may I show you today, sir?'

He gave her a low, hot look. 'There are any number of things I would like to see. But let us limit ourselves to jewellery, Margot. We are in a p-public place, after all.'

She pretended to be shocked. And for a moment, he looked sincerely alarmed to have offended her. Then she laughed, for there was never any real harm in him. And it was clear by his returned smile that she knew he was not laughing at the stammer that sometimes appeared when he said certain words.

They both smiled in silence for a moment, enjoying the easy camaraderie. Then she said, 'Jewellery is all you are likely to be shown. It is all you will get from me, at any rate.'

That had been foolish of her. If she wanted the world to believe that these visits were innocent, she must learn not to encourage the man when he flirted. But it was too tempting not to play along with his little game.

He grinned back at her. 'I must hope, when I find a wife as lovely as you, she will be more agreeable.'

'Oh, I seriously doubt so, Mr Standish. You seem like the sort of man who will be back in my showroom the day after the wedding, buying gifts for your many cousins. I would advise any wife of yours to bar the door against you, until you promise some modicum of fidelity.'

'If you were my wife, I would bar the door myself, with us both inside.' She was sure that he meant it in jest. The idea of him taking her as his wife was quite ridiculous. It was only her overwrought imagination that made the words sound like a sincere offer.

But that did not keep her from dwelling on the scene. The thought of the two of them, locked together in a secluded room gave her a strange, nervous feeling, somewhere between anticipation and fear. She ignored it and gave him a wide-eyed innocent look, as though she could not possibly understand what he meant by such a suggestion. 'But if you locked me up, how would I get to the shop?'

'You would not need to be in this showroom, to show me all the treasure I wished to see,' he pointed out, quite reasonably.

'All the more reason not to marry you then,' she said triumphantly. 'The shop belonged to my father and now it belongs to me. It would be like denying my first love for another, were I to marry you.'

He was still smiling. But it was clear, by his expression, that he did not understand why she would not choose him over her work. She had not really expected him to. It hardly mattered, really. Even if he had been joking about marriage, he assumed it was the ultimate goal of any woman, no matter her station.

All the same, she was quite serious in her love for the shop. It would have been nice had he been the least bit serious about his feelings. But if marriage required that she sacrifice everything she had worked so hard to achieve, it was better that they remain friends.

As it sometimes did, at moments like this, the other likelihood occurred to her. Some day he would suggest an arrangement that had nothing to do with marriage. Late at night when she was lying alone in bed, in the little apartment above the shop, she wondered what her answer to such a question would be. But thinking about the Marquess of Fanworth at bedtime led to the sort of complicated, confusing feelings that had no place in the simple elegance of de Bryun's. Especially not when he was sitting right in front of her and all he wanted was to buy some jewellery.

Now, he gave a theatrical sigh to assure her that the day's flirting was at an end. 'You torment me, Margot, with your unattainable beauty. You do not b-blame a man for trying, I hope.'

'Of course not, Mr Standish. I presume wine and proposals are not the only thing on your mind this morning. Do you wish to look at bracelets? Earrings? Or have you come for the necklace you ordered last week?'

'It is not finished so soon,' he said, amazed. 'The thing you sketched for me was wondrously complicated.'

It had been. All the same, she had refined the design immediately on his leaving the shop and encouraged Mr Pratchet to rush the execution of it. She had set the stones in their places herself, so that she might make sure that there was not even the slightest deviation from her plans. It had been a tricky business. The largest of the stones had a small occlusion which kept it from true perfection. She had considered recutting it, or trying to find a replacement. But the gem had been so perfect in colour and form that she could not resist. Instead, she had chosen to frame the flaw with a tiny cluster of pearls. Now, it was like the beauty spot on the face of an attractive woman. The tiny mark accented the perfection of the rest. The result had been, in her opinion, a masterwork. She was eager for him to see it.

'For you, sir, there must be no waiting.' She gave

a gesture and the shop girl at the door stepped forward with the velvet-lined case, placing it into Margot's hands so she might present it with sufficient ceremony. She undid the latches and offered the open box to her friend with a slight bow of her head. Inside, the red stones glowed with the heat of a beating heart.

His breath caught in anticipation as he took it from her. 'It is more marvellous than I imagined.' He lifted the necklace carefully to the light and it sparkled like frozen fire. 'So clever. So modern in its execution. And yet, respectful of the rank and beauty of the wearer.'

'Pearls are a much more refreshing look than the diamonds you suggested,' she said. 'No one will have a necklace like this.'

'I have never seen one like it,' he admitted. 'And I am sure the lady will be as impressed as I. She has been pining for rubies. Her unhappiness will be quite forgotten, when she sees this.'

Why a woman would have any right to be unhappy when she had the attention of such a man was a mystery to Margot, but she nodded in approval.

There was an awkward pause for a moment, as he smiled at her over the necklace. Then he spoke again. 'You really are an amazing talent, Margot de-de B-Bryun.'

There was another of the slight hesitations in his words that appeared when he was being particularly candid with her. She ignored it, sure that such a great man would have been appalled to demonstrate vulnerability. Tonight, when she remembered the conversation in her mind, she would think of that tiny fault with fondness, or perhaps something even warmer. He was like the ruby at the centre of the necklace he admired, all the more interesting for being slightly less than perfect.

It gave her pause. She was already planning the time before sleep to include thoughts of the Marquess of Fanworth. It was unwise to have such fantasies, even in the privacy of one's own room. Perhaps Mr Pratchet was right. She was encouraging a rake and courting ruin.

When she answered, she made sure that her tone held no significant meaning, other than that of a craftsperson gratified at the recognition of her skill. 'Thank you, sir. It is a great compliment, coming from one who needs as much jewellery as you seem to.'

'I mean it,' he said softly, and with even more conviction. 'Not many jewellers would be able to improve on the original…original idea, that is. You seem to know instinctively what is needed.'

She bowed her head. 'It pleases me that you think I have inherited some small measure of my father's talent.'

'It is more than that, I am sure. You said your father died before you were born.'

'Unfortunately, yes, sir. In a robbery.'

'Then you have taught yourself the skills necessary to honour him.' The marquess nodded in approval. 'It shows a keen mind and an excellent understanding of current styles.' Then he frowned. 'But there was a robbery, you say?' He glanced around him, as though measuring the security of the vault doors against threat.

She smiled and shook her head. 'Not in the shop. He was set upon in the country while delivering stones to a client.'

'You would never take such risks yourself, I hope.'

Since that threat had come from the dead man whose name she had taken such care to remove from the shop window, she was sure that she would not. From now on, there would be no other name on the shop but de Bryun, therefore no risk of villainous partners. 'I take a great deal of care to be sure I am not put in the same situation as my poor father.'

He smiled again. 'That is good to know. But if you find yourself in need of p-protection...' He stopped when he realised how the offer might sound, 'I mean, in need of a strong arm to d-defend you, you must call upon me immediately and I will come to your aid.'

Suddenly, the poised rake who liked to flirt with her seemed totally out of his depth. She understood the feeling. At his offer, her heart had given another inappropriate flutter and she had very nearly sighed aloud. For a moment, it seemed they were both utterly lost in the confusion and hopelessness of their situation. The attraction between them was strong, but she dared not call it love.

When a rich and powerful man became infatuated with a woman so far beneath him, the future was inevitable, and far more like this accidental offer of protection than the earlier offers of marriage.

She gathered her poise and smiled to put him at his ease, again. 'If I am in difficulty, of course I shall seek you out, Mr Standish.' From the outer room, there was the distant ring of a bell and the sound of female voices. Her sister, and her friend Lady Daphne Collingsworth, were enquiring after her, in the main shop.

If they caught her spending too much time with the marquess, they would bother her over it just as Mr Pratchet did. It would be even worse should they suspect how she truly felt. She must bring to-day's meeting to a premature and unwelcome end before she became so foolish as to reveal herself.

She rose, to signify that she had other customers to attend to. 'Thank you so much for your kindness. But as I said, there will be no more robberies. I am perfectly safe.' She held the case out to him and he replaced the necklace. 'Would you like this wrapped? Or perhaps we might deliver it to you.'

He rose as well. 'No need. I will take it now, just as it is. You shall be receiving the balance we agreed upon from my bank, later in the day. When I come again tomorrow morning, you will be here to greet me and will sell me some earrings to match this necklace.'

'You may be sure of it, Mr Standish.' She held open the gauze curtain, so he might exit the salon.

As he passed Justine and Daphne in the main room, his demeanour changed, just as it sometimes seemed to when others were present. His smile was cool and distant and he offered the briefest bow of acknowledgement. He did not so much as look at Margot as she escorted him to the door, signalling a clerk to hold it open as he approached. It was as if their conversation had never taken place. Then he was gone.

Once the shop door closed, Daphne reached out to clutch her arm. 'Fanworth, again?'

'Mr Standish,' Margot said firmly. 'I respect his desire for anonymity.'

Justine looked worriedly out the shop window at the man's retreating back. 'These frequent visits are becoming worrisome, Margot.'

'But the frequent purchases are not,' Margot said in response. 'He is one of my best customers. If he tells others the source of the piece he has just commissioned from me, I expect a sharp uptake in trade.'

'No amount of money will make up for a lost reputation,' Justine said, in a dire tone.

It certainly had in Justine's case. Margot bit back the response. It was horrible and unfair to her poor sister, who had suffered much before finding a man who adored her, despite her unfortunate past.

Instead, she took a deep breath and said, 'I am taking no risks with my reputation. We are in a public place in full view of half-a-dozen people. He comes here to buy jewellery. Nothing more than that.' There was no reason to mention the private jokes, the innuendos, and worst of all, the florid proposals he offered her on an almost daily basis.

'No one needs as much jewellery as he buys,' Justine said, stating the obvious. 'He is a marquess. And you are not just the daughter of a shopkeeper. You are a woman in trade.' Though she had been just that a few short months ago, Justine spoke as if it was something shameful. 'There can be nothing more between you than commerce, Margot. Nothing honourable, at least.'

'I am fully aware of that,' Margot said, in a tired voice. It was a painful truth, but she did not wish to think of it any more.

Justine was staring at her, her gaze holding and searching, as she had when Margot was a child and caught pinching sweets from the kitchen. 'See that you do not forget it. Because I would not wish to see you succumb when he finally makes the offer he is likely to.'

'He would never…' Margot said, trying to sound more sure than she felt.

'Such men are all the same, when it comes to women beneath their class,' Justine answered, just as resolute. 'Though you claim the marquess is amiable and kind, his reputation in the *ton* is quite different. He is the proudest member of an already proud family. His blood is as cold as it is blue and he holds all of society in disdain. He has hardly a word to say to his equals, much less his inferiors.'

'That is not how he acts when he is with me,' she said, wondering what it meant.

'If he behaves differently when he is with you, it is a ruse to weaken your resistance. When he is done toying with you, he will attempt to collect you, just as he has the pretty baubles he comes here to purchase.'

It was more than that. She was sure. Perhaps he did want something more than jewellery. But it had risen out of genuine affection. She was sure when he finally made his offer, it would be more than just a conquest to him. But Justine would not have believed that, had she been witness to his behaviour, only moments ago. He had angled after her shamelessly. And she had allowed it.

She had allowed him to be too forward. If so, he would think less of her. Perhaps he assumed that she was as free with others as she was with him. If that was so, things would end exactly as her sister predicted. He would use her and discard her. She would be lucky if the only damage left in his wake was her broken heart.

For now, she would give the answer her sister wanted to hear. 'I will be on my guard,' Margot said, avoiding her sister's gaze. For if Justine looked at her, and into her soul, she would see the truth that Margot was unable to hide.

She had fallen in love with a man no more attainable than the moon.

Chapter Two

Damn and hell.

If you need pruh-pruh-protection...

What had he been thinking? To use those words made it sound as if he intended a dishonourable offer. Since the lady in question laughed at his offers of marriage, the last thing he needed was for her to think there was some darker, ulterior motive for these visits. And even worse, he had stumbled over the word, making it sound as if he was afraid to say them.

Stammering idiot.

He'd been called that often enough, as a youth. At times like this, he still had to remind himself that it was not accurate. Stammering and idiocy had no link. One could be the first without being the second. One could even control the first, with practice and care.

Stephen Standish, Marquess of Fanworth, strolled through the gauze curtain and back into the regular shop. As always, it was like stepping from a dream of paradise into the harsh light of reality. At the counter stood Miss de Bryun's sister, giving him a disapproving look. The woman was almost an equal in looks to his own dear Margot. More importantly, she was a sister-in-law to the Duke of Bellston.

He returned a look of equal coldness which prevented the need for speech, but offered a barely respectful bow to show he knew of her family connections. To the others in the shop, he offered nothing more than a sweeping, disdainful glance. He felt them shrink ever so slightly in response.

It was not as if any here were likely to address him. They would not dare. But he had grown so used to avoiding conversation of any sort that the attitude came as second nature. Better to let the world assume that you could not be bothered with them, than to call you a fool should your tongue tangle during an unplanned sentence.

He walked down the street, away from the shop, holding his scowl and aloof stare like a shield before him. He was the heir to a dukedom. There was nothing his father or the rest of the world could do about it. That alone was enough to keep him safe and untouched by the opinions of those around him.

But if one refused to speak for fear of embarrassment, one walked alone. It made him miss, all the more, his time in the shop with Margot de Bryun. Who could have guessed a chance encounter with a shopkeeper would have altered his world and his future?

A month ago, he had come into her shop meaning to purchase a trinket for an actress he was planning to seduce. He'd left two hours later with an emerald bracelet in his pocket and the target of his affections totally forgotten.

At first glance, it was the beauty of the woman waiting upon him that had given him reason to pause. Red-gold hair, playful green eyes, and a figure far too perfect to be hidden behind a shop counter. But it was her smile that most affected him. He could not have been more dazzled had he stood on the street and stared directly into the sun.

'May I help you?' she'd said. It might as well have been a choir of angels, for all he heard.

It had made him careless. He'd attempted to be glib.

'Miss de Bryun, I presume?' At least, that was what he'd meant to say. And as usual, when presented with a combination of Bs and Ds and Ps, his speech had failed him altogether. In a moment of profound cowardice, he'd dispensed with his title and given her his surname, hoping that it might still be possible to slink away, unnoticed.

She had not been like some people, when presented with such a disaster. She had not tried to help him by finishing the sentence. Nor had she looked at him with pity. Her smile had not dimmed an iota. Instead, she had waited patiently for her turn. And then she'd purred, 'If you please, Mr Standish. A gentleman who is about to spend as much as you are must call me Margot. Now come into the inner salon and I will pour us a glass of wine. Then you will tell me what it is you desire.'

What did he desire? Her. For ever. From that moment on. It took no great skill to bed a woman, but had it ever been so easy to talk to one? She had questioned him about the taste of the woman he wished to impress and about his own. She did not so much as blink at the pauses in his speech when he struggled for a word. And then she had presented him with a bracelet which she assured him was worthy of the temptress he described.

It was formed as a serpent. Each linked section had been studded with emerald scales. Moonstones were set for eyes. It had been so flexible it had seemed to slither as he held it, almost as if it were alive. The little jaws opened to clamp the tail and hold it closed.

When he'd realised she was the artist responsible for the design, he had questioned her for more than an hour until she'd explained each joint and hinge, and showed him sketches for other works. She had promised to show him the workroom, should he come again. And of course, he had returned, again and again. He had met the craftsman, learned the names of all the tools and expressed such curiosity about all elements of the business that she'd joked he was well on his way to managing the shop himself.

While he had learned much about jewellery making, Margot de Bryun was still a mystery to him. He knew she had a sister, but little more than that. Since she clung adamantly to the de Bryun surname, he doubted that there was a husband waiting in the rooms she occupied above the shop. But might there be a lover, or perhaps a fiancé, ready to greet her when the shop closed?

It did not matter. He might want her to be as sweet and innocent as she appeared on the day he finally found the right words to make her consider his proposal. But even if she was not, he would marry her the moment she agreed.

And if she refused marriage? Then he would dispense with propriety, dazzle her with his rank and wealth, and seduce her, right there on the white velvet of the divan. When she had been loved near to insensibility, she would be much more agreeable to a permanent union. He would wear down her objections and he would have her and keep her.

Generations of breeding informed him everything that was wrong with the situation at hand. He supposed it was the same for Margot, since she treated his advances as little more than playful banter. But common sense informed him, even louder, all the things that were right about such a marriage. He could talk to her. For when would he ever find another woman so perfect?

Society could go hang. She made him happy. And by the smile that lit her face each time he walked in her door, the feeling was mutual. They were in love. They would marry. The rest was not important.

His family was a concern, of course. But he cared no more for the duke's opinion than he did for society. The plan was already in place that would win his mother to his side. Once they had married, and Margot had given up the shop to be his marchioness, her past would be forgotten.

He returned to his apartments with his head full of dreams, only to be dragged back to earth by his butler's announcement. 'Lord Arthur Standish is waiting for you in the drawing room, my lord.'

'Thank you.' Stephen's first impulse had been

to curse in response. His brother was quite good company, in the evenings when they were both the worse for drink. But in broad daylight, it was all too easy to see his flaws. To see him now would tarnish all the pleasure of his visit with Margot.

As expected, he entered the drawing room to find Arthur sprawled in the best chair by the window, a large glass of brandy already to his lips. At the sight of his host, he paused to raise his drink in salute. 'Hail the conquering hero, returned from Montague and de Bryun.'

'Not Montague, any more,' Stephen corrected, moving the brandy decanter to the other side of the room. 'What do you know of my visits there?'

'All of Bath knows of it by now, I am sure.'

'And why is that?' Stephen could guess the answer. He reached past his brother and opened the curtains wide to let in the morning sun.

Arthur groaned at the sudden brightness, grabbed up a decorative pillow from the divan and disappeared behind it. 'How does Bath know of you and the shop girl? I make sure to remark upon it whenever I have a chance.' The empty brandy glass appeared from behind the cushion, waving as if a refill was expected.

Stephen grabbed the pillow and tossed it across the room to fall beside the brandy bottle. 'It is a wonder that anyone listens to you. You are so often in your cups that you are hardly a reliable witness.'

The shaft of light that hit the younger man caused a shudder and a squint. 'I only tell the story to those similarly inflicted.' Then he grinned. 'On holiday, it is not difficult to find people who overindulge in the evenings and then drink their weight in the pump room the next morning hoping for a cure.'

Stephen grunted in response. He was on the verge of losing his temper, and with the excitement would come the stuttering. He fixed his brother with a warning glare.

Arthur paid no attention to it, walking across the room towards the brandy. 'But enough of my flaws. Let us discuss yours.'

Stephen ignored both the drinking and the comment, but redoubled the intensity of his glare.

'How is Miss de Bryun today? As beautiful as always, I assume?'

'It is no concern of yours.'

Arthur pursed his lips and gave a small nod, as if the statement was a confirmation of his suspicions. 'Have you made her your mistress yet? Or does the rest of Bath still stand a chance with her?'

'I have no intention of making her my mistress,' Stephen said, though his body hummed softly at the suggestion. 'And, no, to the second question as well. The lady is virtuous.' He spoke the next slowly, so that Arthur might hear the warning. 'You would do well to remember the fact yourself.'

'All women begin as virgins,' Arthur reminded him. 'But it is easy enough to rectify. Perhaps I shall pay her a visit and discuss the matter.'

This was quite enough. Stephen kept his tone low and menacing, then let each word drop slowly from his mouth, each clear and in the proper order. 'You will regret it. I assure you.'

'Threatening me?' Arthur laughed.

Stephen responded with a grim smile and silence. It was usually enough to set his opponent out of sorts and rendering a hasty apology. But when the man in question was Arthur, there were no guarantees.

'If our father cannot scare me into behaving, then you stand no chance at all. Now, to the matter at hand. You are far too concerned with this girl, Stephen. I quite understand the attraction. She is a beauty. But if you do not have an understanding with her, to be so possessive of her makes no sense. It is not as if you can marry her, after all.'

His impending marriage was not Arthur's business. The comment was not worthy of a response. But silence no longer served to smooth the conversational road. The lack of denial gave away far too much of his future plan.

Arthur noticed it and very nearly dropped his glass in surprise. 'That is not what you intend, is it? You mean to marry her? His Grace will never approve.'

'His Grace can be damned,' Stephen said. Those words, though inappropriate for the scion of the family, never came with difficulty.

'Well, think of the rest of us then,' Arthur said,

looking mildly horrified. 'It will embarrass the entire family if you run off and marry a shop girl. You cannot make someone like that the next Duchess of Larchmont.'

'She is not a shop girl,' Stephen said, a little too sharply. 'She owns the establishment. A different class from us, certainly, but hardly a menial. And once we are married, she will not have a need to keep shop.' He had more than enough money to keep her in jewellery of her own. 'Her sister married a Felkirk,' he added. Once the shop was closed, they would play up the connection to the Duke of Bellston and the marriage would not seem so remarkable.

But Arthur was still so shocked that he put down his glass and gave his full attention to the conversation. 'You truly are serious.' His brother was shaking his head in disbelief. 'You really mean to do it? I understand that you do not listen to Father. The pair of you loathe each other. And what am I but to be ignored? But think of our sister. Her reputation will suffer for this.'

'Her father is Larchmont,' Stephen said, frowning at the mention of their father. 'If she survives that, what harm will my marriage do her?'

'What of Mother? You will break her heart over this.'

'I most certainly will not,' Stephen said. 'Louisa and Margot will be like sisters, once I've introduced them. And I have just the thing to placate Mother.' He reached into his pocket for the jewellery box.

Arthur looked even more shocked. 'You got the duchess a gift from your ladybird's shop?'

'She is not my ladybird,' Stephen said, struggling to maintain his patience. 'And this is not some idle trinket.' He opened the box and produced the necklace. 'It is a replacement for the Larchmont rubies. And it is one of Margot's own creations.' He offered it to his brother, still quite pleased with the result. 'If you do not tell me the thing is magnificent, then you are a liar and I have no time for you. Margot is amazingly talented. I will not hear otherwise.'

Arthur was silent for a moment, then nodded in agreement. 'It is a beautiful thing, to be sure. I am sure Mother would appreciate it.'

'Would?' This doubtful answer sounded almost like his brother meant to add a 'but' to the sentence.

Arthur did not speak for a moment, but took the necklace to the window, squinting again in the brightness, before his eyes adjusted. 'How familiar were you with the necklace that was stolen?'

'Enough to have this made,' Stephen replied. 'It is not as if I spent my youth fishing in Mother's jewel casket, as Louisa did.' He glanced at the necklace in his brother's hands. 'It is close enough, is it not? The stones seem about the right weight. The pearls are new, of course. And the setting is lighter. Still, it is as impressive as the original.'

Arthur gave him a worried look. 'That is not what I mean. I saw the insurance report. It had a description of the stones. There is a flaw in the main one, right near the corner.' He held the necklace up to the light again and the sunlight cast a blood-red shadow through the ruby and on to the floor. 'And this has one as well.' He looked back at Stephen again, sombre this time. 'This is not a close match, Brother. This is the same stone.'

'The one that was stolen?' The necklace in question had been gone for almost two months. It was his mother's sadness at the loss that had brought this idea into his head.

'Taken from the house in Derbyshire,' his brother agreed. 'Strangely enough, the stones found their way into the hands of your Miss de Bryun. If I were a suspicious man, I would think that you had given them to her.'

'Of all the cheek.' Family connections did not give Arthur the right to hurl insults about over something that had to be an innocent mistake.

His brother held up a hand in apology. 'I know that it was not you. Someone sold them to her. If she is responsible for the buying and selling in that shop, she must know the source and, therefore, the thief. It is quite a coincidence that she sells them back to the very family that lost them, is it not?'

'Only that, I am sure.' If Arthur was right about the origin of the stones, it was beyond strange. Margot claimed to choose her stock with care. There was nothing in her manner to suggest that she might be guilty of trading in stolen goods.

And that the family's own jewels should find their way home without some comment from her... 'She knows nothing of my family,' he said, relieved to have found the flaw in Arthur's logic.

His brother responded to this with sceptical silence. 'Do you really suppose that is true? Many people in Bath know who you are, Stephen. You cannot think that a marquess travels unnoticed by society.'

'I make no effort to trade upon the title.' But neither did he act like an ordinary gentleman. When he was not speaking directly with Margot, he behaved just as his father did: as though the rest of the world was far beneath his dignity.

'Surely someone must have remarked upon seeing you there,' his brother said quite reasonably. 'You said yourself that her sister is connected to Bellston.'

He had seen the sister more than once and she had acknowledged him as if she knew perfectly well who he was. Had he expected her to remain mum on the identity of the man visiting her shop? She must have told her sister. 'Even if she knows who I am...'

'Then it is still an amazing coincidence that she put these very stones back into your hands. How much did she charge you for them, I wonder?'

A small fortune. But considering the reason for the necklace, he had not thought twice. 'I was the one who requested rubies,' he said. But a clever criminal might have led him to the idea before he'd even noticed.

'I suspect she had a good laugh about it, once you were gone from the shop,' his brother replied gently, placing one hand on his shoulder and returning the necklace to him with the other.

'She would not.' She would not dare. If he did not allow the Duke of Larchmont to make sport at his expense, he certainly would not take it from a Bath shopkeeper.

Or there might be an explanation. There had to be. If not, he had been behaving like a mooncalf over a heartless jade. And all because she had not laughed in his face when he spoke.

Arthur continued, unaware of his darkening mood. 'Well, in any case, thank God we discovered the ruse before you had given this to Mother.

She would have recognised the stones immediately, I am sure. And Father...'

He did not need to finish. They both knew what would have happened. His father would have proclaimed that his heir was an idiot, just as he did every time they met. It was why they no longer spoke.

'If what you say is true, Larchmont will never hear of it.' If Margot de Bryun proved false, he would see that she was punished, as she deserved. Then he would distract himself with any number of females who were too awed by his rank and temper to comment upon his flaws. The whole mess would be buried and forgotten before his parents arrived later in the month so that the duke could take the waters for his gout.

'Let me handle this,' Arthur said, his voice still soft with understanding. 'We will show the stones to an enquiry agent. If I am right, than he can go to the shop and take her into custody.'

'Certainly not.' Perhaps the girl had made a fool of him. Or perhaps there was still some perfectly innocent explanation for the reappearance of the stones. But if there was a decision to be made, he would do it himself. His heart was not so tender that it needed coddling. Nor would he endure, for another moment, the pitying look his wastrel brother was giving him now.

He glared back at Arthur until he felt his brother yield, as a dog might when it saw a wolf. Then he spoke. 'I will take the stones to your enquiry agent, so they might be identified. Then I will deal with the shopkeeper.'

Chapter Three

Margot stared out the window of the shop, leaning her elbows on the glass case in front of her. She would never have allowed such slack behaviour from the people in her employ. But they were not as dejected as she was, after another day alone in the shop.

Lord Fanworth had not come yesterday, as he had promised when their conversation had been interrupted. She'd hoped he'd at least visit long enough to tell her how the necklace had been received. She liked to be told that her designs made others happy.

Of course, if the happiness meant that her Stephen Standish was currently entwined in the arms of some ruby-bedazzled Cyprian, she was not so sure she wanted to know. It was foolish of her to be so obsessed with a man who spent so much of his time buying jewellery for his lovers. But to her, the time they spent together, just talking, was more valuable than anything he had purchased at her shop. Surely he must realise that true affection could not be bought with rubies.

Once again, the worrisome thought occurred to her. Her sister and Mr Pratchet were right. He had seduced her mind, convincing her that she was more important to him than the other women he courted. On the day he finally asked for her body, she would give herself freely, without a second thought. It would be the death of her reputation, if they were not very discreet. But to refuse would mean that she would never know his touch. To imagine such a future was intolerable.

Of course, it might be the only alternative available. He had not come yesterday. Today was almost through and there had been no sign of him, either. One more day and it would be longer than any interruption since the first day he had found her. How long could one stay in bed? It was another question she did not want an answer to. If he gave even a hint of what he had been doing, it would surely make her cross. Assuming he came back at all.

Perhaps these visits meant nothing to him. Or perhaps their interaction was becoming too expensive. The ruby necklace had been very dear. Even the pockets of a marquess must have some limit to their depth. But he must realise he did not need to make a purchase to command her attention. She would have happily poured out the wine and invited him to sit and rest himself. Anything to have him here, for even a few minutes, to lighten her spirit and ease the passing of the day.

It was not as if she did not enjoy her shop. But at some point in the last month, she had come to think of the marquess as a part of her day. His absence was like coming to the tea tray and finding the pot empty.

Not quite. At least one knew that there would be more hot water and a few leaves left in the bottom of the tin. But suppose India ceased to exist and there were to be no more tea ever? Or, worse yet, that the tea had simply gone back to London, or to somewhere even further?

Or to someone else?

It was all the more troublesome that she could not share her fears with those around her. Her sister would remark that it served her right for growing accustomed to those unnatural visits. Mr Pratchet would inform her that it was for the best. Even now, she could sense him lingering in the doorway of the workroom, trying to catch her attention.

She turned and caught him squarely in her gaze. 'Is there something I might help you with, Mr Pratchet?'

'If you are not too busy.' He glanced behind him, as if to indicate that their discussion was better unheard by the small group of customers already in the shop.

She sighed and walked towards him into the back room, shutting the door behind her.

When he was sure that he could not be heard, he announced, 'The Marquess of Fanworth has not visited in almost a week.'

'Only two days,' she said, without thinking.

His eyebrows rose. 'It is a great relief to me that he seems to be losing interest. If he returns, you must not encourage him. People will talk.'

'I must not encourage him?' Margot laughed. 'He is a customer, Mr Pratchet. I certainly hope people talk about his presence here. If people of a certain class notice that we get regular trade from the son of the duke, they will come here as well.' And if, just once, he should give one of her pieces to a member of his family, rather than wasting them on opera dancers, there was no telling how much trade might result.

'I do not like it, all the same.' There was something in Pratchet's tone that was more than concern for a vulnerable young woman. This sounded rather like jealousy.

Oh dear.

It was happening again, just as it had with Mr Perkins and Mr Jonas. He was becoming too familiar. He was acting as if he had any right to control her personal behaviour, as if she were just some woman and not the person who paid his salary. If it was not nipped in the bud immediately, she would be placing an ad for a new goldsmith within the week. 'I fail to see what your opinion has to do with the workings of this shop,' she said, using a voice that should remind him of his place.

Rather than take the tone as the warning it was meant to be, Mr Pratchet ruffled his feathers. 'It need have nothing to do with the shop at all. I will not see you damage your reputation for base profit. You are a lady and must take care.'

'I am your employer,' she said and waited for him to realise his mistake.

'One does not preclude the other,' he said, still oblivious. 'If we are to have an understanding—'

'Clearly, we do not understand each other at all,' she said, cutting him off. 'Not if you think you have a right to dictate to me.'

He seemed surprised at the interruption, 'You would be wise to listen to me.' It was as if he was scolding an unruly child. 'You could not manage the shop alone. You have some talent for design, I'll admit…'

'Thank you,' she said in a way that should have put him on his guard.

'But you know nothing of working in metal.'

'I know enough to appraise the talent in a goldsmith. It was why I hired you,' she said. 'And why I pay you handsomely for your skill.'

'But if we are to enter into a more enduring partnership, for example a marriage...'

'Marriage?' she said, glacial.

He blundered on. 'You mentioned, when you brought me on, that there might be a chance to be a partner in the shop. What better way to establish such a partnership then with the most permanent alliance?'

'What better way?' She laughed out loud at this. 'Why, with lawyers, of course. And an exchange of money, from you to me. At such time as I consider taking on a partner...a junior partner,' she corrected, 'there will need to be contracts and negotiations on both sides. I will expect you to buy a share of the business, just as you would if I were a man.'

'But you are not a man,' he said, as though she might need to be reminded.

'I do not intend to marry you, simply to secure a partner for my business. With the current matrimonial laws in this country, that would be little better than handing you the keys to the front door and walking away.'

'There is nothing wrong with the law,' he said. 'It is just as God intended.' By the long steady look he gave her, it was clear that he thought any problems lay not with the state, but with the woman in front of him.

'I will discuss the matter with God, when I meet him,' she said. 'But that will not be for a good many years. And when he greets me, he will still be calling me Miss de Bryun.'

The pronouncement was probably blasphemy. But it was clear by Mr Pratchet's shocked silence that he finally believed she was in earnest.

She continued. 'You have been labouring under a misapprehension about your future here. I hope I have corrected it. If I have not? As your employer, I am well within my rights to let you go, no matter how good your work might be. But one thing I am most assuredly not going to do is marry you, Mr Pratchet.'

'Yes, Miss de Bryun.' The answer was respectful, but there was something in his expression that did not match the agreeable tone. He seemed to be recalculating, like a chess player who had found another path to mate. When he spoke again, it was in a more humble voice, though there was no apology in his words. 'All the same, I stand by my warning to you about the Marquess of Fanworth. Do not trust him, or his family. I am sure what he intends for you is more than a simple transaction. If he is no longer coming to the shop, then you are lucky to be rid of him. And now, if you will excuse me, there is work to attend to.' He turned and walked away.

As Margot went back to the main salon, she realised that she had just been dismissed from her own workshop. She sighed. It did no good to become preoccupied over the mysterious marquess, if it meant that she was not paying attention to more important matters. The erosion of her authority over Mr Pratchet should be foremost in her mind. One more such unusual outburst and she would have to let him go, for both their sakes. She would give him a letter of reference, of course. He did excellent work. In a shop run by a man, he would be no trouble at all.

But she had no intention of allying herself to a

man who thought he could choose who she did or did not talk to, or who thought that a marriage was the next logical step after a position as an underling.

The idea left her in such a mood she barely remembered to smile in welcome as a customer came into the shop. He waved away the assistance of the nearest clerk, but remained at the front counter, staring thoughtfully down at a tray of inexpensive rings. Then he removed a pair of spectacles from his pocket and consulted a small notebook, nodding to himself and making notes with the stub of pencil that was tied to the binding.

Margot paused to assess him. Something was wrong about his demeanour. She could tell by the cut of his coat that he could afford something much better than the work he was admiring. But the style of his garments was simplistic to the point of anonymity. She almost expected to see a clerical collar flopping over the lapels and not an ordinary neckcloth.

To a seller of fine jewellery, he was disappointingly unornamented. There was no chain or fob on his waistcoat, no stickpin in coat or cravat, and his buttons were polished ebony to match the fabric of the coat. His only vanity was a gold ring worn on the left hand.

How strange. With no sign of a signet or stone, it looked almost like a wedding ring. She had never seen one on a man before. But one look at it and she was sure that it was a gift from a woman. A fellow who chose to wear such a thing must be a romantic. If so, he should show his devotion to the lady with a purchase of some kind.

'May I help you, sir?' Margot stepped forward with her most brilliant smile.

'You might if you are Miss Margot de Bryun,' he said, giving her an equally charming of smile. There was something behind it that was quite different from the expressions of the men who were usually trying to capture her attention. He gave the impression that he knew more than he was likely to tell.

Her own smile never faltered. 'I am she. But I am sure any of the staff can help you, if you wish to make a purchase.'

'Oh, I am quite sure that they cannot.' His smile

grew even more secretive as he reached into his pocket and produced a neatly lettered card.

E. A. Smith
Problems solved. Objects found.
Private enquiries handled with discretion.

She looked at him again, losing the last of her shopkeeper's courtesy. 'What sort of problems do you solve, Mr Smith?'

'If I told you, I would hardly claim to handle my enquiries with discretion.'

'But you can tell me what brings you here to seek out me, specifically.'

He nodded. 'In this case, the problem is missing jewellery. The owner would like the item returned and the person who took it remanded to the authorities.'

'You are a thief taker?'

He shrugged. 'Sometimes. In this case, you must tell me.' He reached into his pocket and removed a carefully folded piece of paper. 'I am searching for a particular necklace. It belongs to the Duchess of Larchmont.'

She stifled a gasp. The mother of the Marquess of Fanworth. Her Mr Standish had spoken of a woman who missed her rubies. Had he been asking her to design a necklace for a duchess? She struggled to compose herself and examined the drawing. 'It is lovely, but I have nothing of the sort here in this shop.'

Mr Smith looked at her carefully, as though he had some reason to doubt the story. 'It is quite possible that the stones were removed from the setting and sold separately. Perhaps they have already been reset.'

She risked a nod. When ridding oneself of such a distinctive piece, it would be the most sensible thing to do. She waited for Mr Smith to explain himself.

He was looking at her with an equally curious expression. 'Do you deal in rubies, Miss de Bryun?'

His continual questions were growing tiresome. 'We deal in many stones, sir. Rubies are among them. But we do not deal in stolen merchandise, if that is what you are asserting.'

'Perhaps, if you were to look more closely at the stones, you might be able to help me find them.

I have a list of their weights and qualities.' He pushed the paper across the counter towards her.

She felt a cold chill on her neck, before even looking at the sheet. The man was so calm, so assured, and so carefully avoiding any hint of accusation that his visit seemed all the more ominous.

The sketch was followed with a detailed description of the stones: their carat weight, colour and grade. Two stones, emerald cut, one half-carat each, perfect. Two more at a carat, pear-shaped, also perfect. And the largest centre stone, almost two carats by itself, with a little flaw at the corner.

All her previous denials were for nothing. She knew these stones. She'd reset them herself and given them to Stephen Standish. But how had they come to be in her possession? And what was to happen to her now? Most importantly, how was she to explain to Stephen that she had sold his family's gems back to him?

Unless he already knew.

Once the thought had entered her head, it pushed out all others. The stones had been in his family for generations. Surely he had recognised them from the first. Why had he said nothing to her? Had he been the one to send this man? To what purpose?

She was doing him an injustice by doubting him. He might be as innocent of this as she was. Or he might be in some trouble over this that she did not fully understand. Until she had spoken to him about the necklace, she would not be sure.

If she blurted what little she did know to this stranger, she might make matters worse for him and not better. What good would it do to declare her innocence, only to shift the blame and the disgrace on to the man she loved?

She stared down at the description of the rubies, doing her best to keep her face impassive. 'I have no such stones at this time.'

'Should we look in your locked room? Perhaps you might have forgotten.'

'I am not likely to forget stones of this size. But if you insist.' She led him to the room at the back of the shop, taking the key from the chain around her neck. Once inside, she removed the velvet-lined trays that held the loose stones to show him that they were indeed devoid of the things he was looking for.

He did not seem as surprised as he should have, if he'd truly expected to find them there. 'You are sure you have not seen these stones before?'

It was a cleverly phrased question and one that she could not lie through so easily. It hinted that he knew exactly where the stones were and was awaiting her confession. 'Do you doubt my word?'

By the flash of triumph in his eyes, she had given him the answer he expected. 'I only know what I have learned from others. The name of your shop was mentioned in relation to the disappearance of the stones. It is why I have come to ask you about them.'

Her shop? Maybe Stephen had nothing to do with it. Her mind raced. Perhaps it had happened while Mr Montague was still alive. If he had been in the habit of buying stolen property, there was no telling how much of her current stock was compromised. How many such mistakes might she have to apologise for? And would all the people involved be as understanding as Mr Smith seemed?

Perhaps it was not so dire as that. But she would not know until she had searched the records and learned what she could about the rubies. But for Stephen's sake, and her own, it would be wise to wait until she had learned all she could on the subject, before speaking to Mr Smith. 'I know nothing of stolen necklaces,' she said. 'Nor do I understand why anyone would accuse me of such a thing.'

'Let me explain the situation to you.' Mr Smith gave her a sad, almost understanding smile. 'You asked me earlier if I was a thief taker. I must tell you, in some cases, I would most prefer not to be. There are times when one has been led astray, or misinformed, or trusted those that were unworthy. Though they had no intention of breaking the law, those people find themselves in a great deal of trouble. They might be imprisoned, or even hung for a single mistake. But all it would take to avoid the difficulty is to admit the whole truth and return the stones to their rightful owner.'

'If I had the stones, I should most certainly return them,' she said, for that was perfectly true. Then she followed it with half a lie. 'If I see them in the future, I will contact you immediately.'

'That would be wise,' he agreed. 'I will give you

a few days to think on the matter. Then I will return to see if you have anything to tell me.'

'Of course, Mr Smith.' She gave him her most co-operative smile. If the Duke of Larchmont wished to see her hang, innocence would not be enough to protect her. But she could swallow her pride and go to Justine with the story. The Felkirk family was more than strong enough to shield her from Mr Smith and his threats. 'If I discover anything, I shall most assuredly tell you.'

'Until then, good day, Miss de Bryun.' He gave a slight respectful bow and exited the shop.

For a moment, Margot was frozen in place, unsure of what to do next. Then she glanced around her to be sure that the other customers in the shop had been too preoccupied to hear any of the exchange between herself and the thief taker. When she was sure that not even the nearest clerk had eavesdropped, she hurried to the little office she kept at the back of the workroom.

Once there, she brought down the account books, tracing her fingers down lines of sales until she found the records of shipments taken in.

And there was a purchase of loose stones large enough to hide the Larchmont rubies.

Had the merchant passed the stones on to her? The man was a gypsy, but well connected, and the natural son of an earl. She'd never had reason to be suspicious of him before. But then, she'd never been accused of dealing in stolen merchandise.

She went to the files and found the detailed inventory of the purchase. It had been checked in by Mr Pratchet, the description of the gems written in his tidy hand. They were mostly opals, this time, and a nice selection of emeralds. It appeared that she'd had the best of a shipment from the Americas: Brazil, perhaps. And there, at the bottom of the list, were the rubies. Their description was identical to the one that Mr Smith had just shown her.

The pure red of those stones could only have come from Burma. What were they doing with Brazilian emeralds? Mr Pratchet had paid out more than she'd expected to spend on that order. But the amount listed for the rubies was less than a tenth of their actual value. The ink on the line did not seem to match the rest, as though the last item had been added as an afterthought. The total below it had been carefully altered to include the amount paid out for the stolen stones.

She stared at the books for what seemed like hours, trying to understand how she had not noticed before. But hadn't Pratchet just demonstrated how careless she had become while fawning over the Marquess of Fanworth?

When the senior clerk, Jasper, came to her for permission to shut the shop, she gave an absent nod. The sun was near to setting. The other clerks had already gone home to their tea and the building had grown dark and quiet. She followed the boy out into the shop and locked the door the minute he was thorough it. Then she hurried back to the workroom.

If there was an explanation to any of this, it would lay with Pratchet. She went straight to the desk he used as a workbench and searched the drawers, not sure what she expected to find. More stolen gems? Thank God, there were none. Perhaps he was not responsible, after all. He might have been gulled, just as she had been, when presented with a fine bunch of loose stones and a price too good to resist.

But then she turned to the box of scrap gold on the floor beside the table, waiting to be melted and recast. It took only a few moments' prodding to find the setting for the duchess's rubies lying twisted and empty at the bottom.

'What are you doing there?' Mr Pratchet was standing in the doorway, watching as she rifled his workspace.

'What are you still doing here?' she said. For a moment, irrational instinct took her and her eyes darted around the room, searching for a defensive weapon.

'I forgot to take my coat…' As he stared at the broken necklace in her hand, his voice trailed away, reminding her that such fear was overblown. He might be a thief, but he was an unprepossessing specimen who would not further risk his livelihood by attacking her.

'You know what I am doing.' She held the setting out in front of her, so that there could be no denying. 'Explain this.'

'You will not like what I have to tell you,' he

said, stepping forward, unthreatening but un-
afraid.

'There is no doubt of that,' she said. 'You used
me and my shop to trade in stolen materials.'

'Only once,' he replied, as though it should matter.

'And the one time you were caught in it. An
enquiry agent has been here today, searching for
the necklace. What am I to tell him?'

'I warned you of the dangers in dealing with the
marquess,' Pratchet said, as though it were somehow her fault that they had come to this.

'What has he to do with it?' she asked, afraid of
the answer. 'Other than that he came to the shop
looking for rubies, only to have me sell him his
own gems. And how am I to explain that?'

'You won't need to explain it,' Pratchet said.
'He already knows.'

'He does not.' Her heart sank. He had not so
much as batted an eye on taking the stones back.
But then, her sister had always warned her that
attractive men were often the most skilled liars.

'You are naïve, Margot,' said Pratchet, in a voice
he probably thought was kind. In truth, it was no

less patronising than the tone he had used to discuss marriage. 'Have you not wondered how I came by the stones?'

'I assume the thief sold them to you.'

'But why did the thief choose this shop and not some London Lombard merchant? And why did I succumb so easily to the temptation?'

'I have no idea what your motives might be. Perhaps he knew you to be a habitual criminal.' She wanted that to be true. But he had said that this was an isolated occurrence and she believed him. Even now that he was caught, there was nothing in his nature that seemed suspicious.

His face was as bland as it ever was, offering no sign of subterfuge. In fact, he was looking at her with pity. 'I took the stones because I feared giving offence to the man who held them. I had no idea he would report them as stolen, or that his family would send the law to this shop to harass you over them.'

'Are you claiming that the marquess himself gave them to you?'

'I gave my word as a gentleman to say nothing of the truth to anyone,' he said. 'But I did the best to warn you that such a close association with a man like Fanworth was unwise. You cannot understand the motives of the nobles in their great houses. Perhaps it is all an attempt to gain the insurance money while keeping the stones for themselves.'

There was a perverse logic in it. To have a new necklace made would be one way to hide beloved heirlooms in plain sight.

'The fact that he involves you in his schemes is particularly worrying,' Pratchet continued, although she had not asked for his opinion on the matter. 'Since you are young, lovely and unprotected by marriage, I think we can draw the obvious conclusion as to his real motives.'

He made it sound as if those qualities rendered her one step from stupidity. Or perhaps that was what he thought of all women. 'Until I have spoken to Lord Fanworth on the subject, I will not know what to think.' But she did not wish to speak to him, ever again. The truth was likely to ruin everything.

Mr Pratchet let out an incredulous laugh. 'You mean to speak to him? It is clear that the family does not want to admit their part in the disappearance. To call attention to it will only anger them. And to admit that you held the stones…' Pratchet shook his head. 'If you go to him over this, he will have you arrested. Or he will make the unsavoury offer he has been planning all along.'

'I refuse to believe that.' But she could not manage to sound as sure as she had been. Hadn't her sister offered the same warning? But she had been too flattered by Fanworth's visits to heed.

Mr Pratchet gave her another pitying look. 'When you are proven wrong, come to me. Perhaps, if you are married, he will leave you alone. Together we might find a way out of the mess you have created for yourself.' He went to the corner, collected the forgotten coat and went out into the street.

The mess she had created? It was true. She had convinced herself that the Marquess of Fanworth would stoop to be interested in a shopkeeper. Now, she would need to go to Justine and beg her to solve a problem created by her own vanity.

But she would not forget Pratchet's part in this disaster. He had bought the stones and kept the truth from her. If anyone deserved to be gaoled, it was him. But despite his protests of a gentleman's agreement, he could prove in court that she'd had no knowledge of the provenance of the rubies she'd sold. She would pretend to overlook his crime, for the moment, at least. If she sacked him as he deserved, he might disappear just when he was needed to swear to her innocence.

She stared down at the twisted metal still in her hand that had once held such magnificent stones. It was a sad end to see it thrown away as scrap. But it would be even worse if she lost her livelihood over a piece of jewellery.

In the front room, the bell of the shop door rang. Pratchet had not locked it when he'd gone. Without thinking, she stepped to the doorway and called, 'I am sorry, the shop is closed for the evening.'

'Not to me.' The voice was familiar, and yet not so. While she had heard him speak a hundred times, he had always been kind. Never before had she heard him use so cold a tone. Nor would she have thought it possible that three words could be imbued with such calculating, deliberate threat.

Framed in the entrance was the Marquess of Fanworth. And he was staring at the gold in her hand.

Chapter Four

Even as the evidence mounted, Stephen could not help wishing that it was a simple, easily explained mistake.

The enquiry agent had positively identified the stones. There was no question of their identity. Stephen had written to his mother to assure her that the rubies were safe in the family again and would be returned to her when she came to Bath at the end of the month.

But that did not explain what Margot de Bryun had to do with any of it. Arthur claimed that the answer was obvious. Meaning, Stephen supposed, that he was as big an idiot as Father had always claimed. He had been duped by a pretty face and refused to believe the truth even when he could hold the evidence in his hand.

Stephen had stared, frowning at his brother, until the speculation had stopped. Arthur was always willing to see the worst in people, for he was the most cynical creature alive.

Then, he had sent the enquiry agent to speak to Margot directly. Mr Smith returned to say that Miss de Bryun had denied all knowledge of the gems. But there was no chance she would not have recognised them by the description he had given to her. In his opinion, feigned ignorance was little better than a lie and a sign of culpability on her part. A professional opinion from Smith was far more worrisome than Arthur's accusations.

But damn it all, Stephen knew Margot de Bryun and was willing to swear that there was not a calculating bone in her body. And a luscious body it was. He would go to her himself and settle this small misunderstanding about the rubies. If she was innocent, then things would go back to the way they had been.

And if she was guilty?

He hoped, for her sake, that she was not.

Stephen would not know until he saw evidence

with his own eyes, and not just assumptions and suppositions. He'd waited, all afternoon, hoping that she would come forward and explain herself, after Smith's visit. But there had been so sign of her.

Perhaps she truly did not know his name or direction. Or perhaps she was avoiding him. If he wanted the truth, he must go to her and get it.

Dusk was falling as he was walked down Milsom Street towards de Bryun's. It was later than he'd ever visited. It must be closed, or nearly so. But it would give them a chance to speak in private. He was sure she would be the last one out of the door in the evening, for she had but to climb the stairs and be home. When he arrived at the shop, the front room was dark and the sign turned to read 'Closed'. But there was still a glow of light coming from the doorway of the workroom.

On an impulse, he tried the door and felt the handle turn. Not totally closed, then. The bell that rang as he opened was unnaturally loud in the silence of the empty room. When night fell, the cheerful elegance was replaced with a ghostly hush, made even more eerie by the gauze-framed doorways.

Margot de Bryun stepped through the sheer curtains, uttering the standard apology to a customer that had come too late. Then she recognised him and froze, framed in the doorway.

His beautiful Margot, in her simple white gown, was surrounded in a halo of candlelight and holding the empty setting that had once held the Larchmont rubies.

'My Lord Fanworth.' She dropped into a curtsy, as humble and submissive as any shop clerk that had ever waited upon the son of a duke.

The sight turned his stomach.

Idiot. Dolt. Worthless fool.

The words echoed in his mind as they had since he had been old enough to understand their meanings. But this time they were true. Damn his feeble wits. He had trusted her as if she'd been a part of his own body. Now he saw the truth. She knew him. She knew the rubies. Yet she'd said nothing. She'd let him stammer and flirt. She had pretended to laugh with him. But all the while he had been the butt of the joke. The whole time, she had been waiting for the right moment to spring the trap and prove him for the fool he was.

He ignored her beauty, staring through her as if it would be possible to see the black heart beating in that admirable bosom. From this moment on, she would see no more weakness in him. He would see her punished for what she had done. And then he would see her no more. 'How long have you known my title?'

'Since the first,' she said, in a whisper.

'Yet you said nothing.'

She shook head, bracing herself against the doorframe as though she needed support to hide the trembling in her body. 'It was not my place to question you.'

'Neither should you have sold me my own mother's stolen rubies.'

'I swear, I did not know.' Her eyes were round, luminous coins in the firelight. If he was not careful, the soft side of him that had allowed her to lead him by the nose would be believing this story as well. She had lied once. She would do it again.

He stepped forward and snatched the twisted gold from her hand. Arthur might fault him for

not recognising the stones, but on this part of the
necklace he had no doubt. The prongs that had
held the gems canted at weird angles where they'd
been pried away. A few of the surrounding diamonds still remained, but most were like so many
empty eye sockets staring back from around the
gaping wounds that had contained rubies.

'Do you wish the money back? I will get it for
you this instant.' Her voice was weird, distant.
But he was lost in all the times he had seen the
necklace on his mother. How happy it had made
her. How devastated would she be to see it now?

'I need no money.'

'Then I will reset the stones, as they were. Simply bring them back and—'

'You will not touch them again!'

He heard the gasp, as the words hit her like a
whiplash. It was exactly what she deserved for ru-
ining something so beautiful, treating it as nothing more than scrap.

'Then what do you wish of me?' she said, taking a deep breath to steady herself as she waited
for his response.

What did he want from her? If the stones were

reset, there would still be the memory of what had happened to them and how he had behaved, in this very room, mooning over her like a love-sick boy even as she had tricked him. No amount of money would erase such a thing.

'Your Mr Smith was here today, threatening me with gaol or worse,' she said, softly. 'I beg you, my lord, there is no need. You have the stones. You have the setting. Keep the new setting as well. If you will not take it from me, I will return the money you paid for it to your bank, the minute it opens in the morning.'

It was not enough. Reparation would not make him feel any less a fool. Nor would it bring back the time he had spent with her, or the feeling of easy conversation that he'd imagined could go on for ever.

But sending her to gaol would be like throwing roses on a dung heap. It was wasteful. Even now, the thought of her youth and beauty fading in a lightless cell made him feel guilty, not triumphant. God had not designed such a perfect creature to be hidden away and allowed to rot.

'Please,' she said urgently. 'There must be something. If you will not consider my reputation, think of the people who work under me. If you send me away, they will lose their livelihoods. They are totally innocent in this.'

They were innocent. Which meant, he supposed, that she was not.

'What can I do to make this right?' she said, her voice turning desperate. 'Name the thing and you shall have it.'

Without thinking, he stepped closer to her.

She backed away.

It was hardly a surprise. The days of easy camaraderie were over. Stephen Standish might have missed it, but the Marquess of Fanworth felt a grim pleasure to see her shrink before him. She had just offered him anything he wanted. It had been stupid of him to love her. But the very real, very physical desire he felt for her had not changed.

He had thought she was sweet and innocent. But of course, she lied. He continued to advance on her, feeling the flutter of chiffon as they passed into the back salon where they had spent so much time chatting together. It was even darker than the front room had been. The faint haze from the workroom candle cast little more than an eerie glow.

'Anything?' He reached out and touched her face with the tip of her finger. Let her offer, then. She was just as beautiful as ever. Though he might be no smarter, he was not blind. He could stop wanting her. Even if he closed his eyes, he would see her, all the more desirable because he should not have her. The lust rose in his heart, dark and thick as treacle.

At his touch, she was still. She neither shuddered nor flinched. When she spoke, her voice was as cool and businesslike as any whore. 'If I do what you are most likely suggesting, do you promise that I will be safe from gaol, safe from the gallows? That I will keep my reputation...'

'For all that is worth,' he said with a sneer.

She ignored the insult. 'And my shop and the people who work here will be safe from persecution?'

'I care not for them, or the shop. My quarrel is with you.' He stroked her face, letting his fingertips linger on her cheek before settling under her chin, touching her throat. She was as soft and smooth as he had imagined she'd be. When he withdrew, a whiff of bergamot seemed to follow his hand, as though trying to draw him back.

'How many times?'

For a moment, he did not understand. And then, he did and the answer was stunned out of him. The sweet creature he had chatted with in daylight was haggling over the use of her body, now that the sun was down. How could she be so cold and fearless, so masculine, when faced with the loss of her alleged virtue? Perhaps her virtue was not as valuable to her as the shop he sought to protect.

'How many times, my lord?' she repeated. 'How many times must I lie with you to be free of this?' Her eyes narrowed.

'Five,' he said, pulling a number out of the air. 'Once for each stone.'

'Four,' she countered. 'My maidenhead should be worth twice as much, since I have but one to barter with.'

He barked with laughter, even though there was nothing the least bit funny about it. 'Four, then.'

'Four times,' she said, staring coldly back at

him. 'After that, swear that I need never see or
hear from you or your family, ever again. Swear
on your honour as a gentleman. For all that is
worth,' she added, throwing his own insult back
at him.

Never to see her again. For a moment, something stirred in him, like an eel in deep water.
He'd had such hope for their future. But that had
been lost the moment he'd walked into this shop
and seen her holding what was left of the pride
of the Larchmonts. The sweet girl he'd wanted
was an illusion, just as his easy speeches to her
had been. 'I swear,' he said, 'you will never see
me again.'

He reached for the gold setting in her hand, took
it and slipped it into his pocket. Then, he reached
for her. Women were all alike. Four times would
be enough to rid himself of this madness. She
was as beautiful in candlelight as she was in daylight. He had lain with beauties before and their
company became tiresome after the excitement
of courtship was through.

But those women had not been as dangerous as
this one. It would be safer to sleep with a viper

than to be with a woman capable of such duplicity. The risk held its own sort of excitement.

He was standing so close to her now that his skin tingled in awareness of their first kiss. She stared back at him, defiant. Good. He did not want a weeping virgin trying to make him guilty for a reparation that was far gentler than the punishment she deserved.

He closed the last inch between them and their lips met. The kiss was exquisite. Not cherries or strawberries. They were both too sweet. Blackcurrant, perhaps. Tart, complex as wine, her lips closed around his tongue, her teeth grazed it as if she wished to bite.

His balls tightened in his breeches.

How long had he been dreaming of taking her, right here on the white-velvet divan? His fantasies had been innocent compared to this. He had not imagined this helpless feeling of abandon as her body touched his. She fit perfectly against him, the curve of her hip in his hand, her belly cradling his erection. He ran his hand over the bare skin of her shoulder, circling to the back of her neck so that he might press her mouth to his. Such a delicate nape, fringed with the soft hair he had longed to stroke. He rubbed it with his knuckle and her lips opened even wider, eager for him.

One kiss, and she was driving him mad. He wanted to ravish her with his mouth, mark her with his kisses, to claim her body as his own.

If he felt so about an innocent touch, how would he survive a more intimate one? He experimented, sliding a fingertip inside her bodice to seek her nipple. Finding, pinching, kneading the whole breast, a match for his cupped palm.

Her throat arched and her breath caught, and she whimpered like a hungry kitten. She wanted more.

The response flashed through him like heat lightning. He'd been mistaken. Four times would not be enough. Not four hundred, or four thousand. What she had done did not matter, compared to the need he felt for her after a few simple touches. He kissed his way down her throat, making her arch backward in his arms, easing her to the couch so he might kiss his way down the graceful hollows of her neck and shoulders.

Her legs spread wide. One rested on the floor,

the other bent at the knee, foot resting on the upholstery. He knelt between them, pushing her skirt up and out of the way. He leaned over her, his mouth suckling an exposed breast, his hand on her calf. Smooth curves, a seemingly endless expanse of silk-encased flesh. He was an explorer on his way to an undiscovered country.

'No.' Suddenly she shuddered under him, pushed away, and rolled off on to the floor, scrambling to be free of him.

It was the most wonderful mistake she had ever made.

When she had seen him, staring at her from the front of the shop, she had known their innocent flirtation was at an end. All that was left was the reckoning that had been predicted by everyone around her.

Had he ever felt anything for her, other than lust? It did not seem so, tonight. In return, she would feel nothing.

She refused to feel fear, if that was what he wanted from her. And hatred was too much like passion. She felt nothing. And she spoke from the emptiness, with her offer.

It amused him. He responded. She negotiated. He accepted.

Then he approached.

If what he was doing with her was a punishment, then perhaps she was one of those poor souls who thrived on abuse. His touch had been like a feather stroke, awakening her appetite.

But cravings could be resisted. She would yield her body, but not her mind. And not her heart.

Then his lips touched hers.

A taste was not enough. She was starving for him, desperate for the kiss. To feel nothing was impossible, with his lips on hers. Anger, then. Hatred. But the rage fed the flames and she raked his tongue with her teeth.

His finger played at the top of her gown.

She pushed her breast into his hand and was rewarded for her boldness. Her dress was open, his hands on her breasts, and then his lips. He was possessing her, making her body his own.

And she wanted him to do it. She was on her back, spreading her legs to make it easier as he gripped her ankle and raised her skirt. Her nipples grew between his teeth. Her legs were wet. And everything inside her ached and trembled, begging for him to hurry, to finish, to take her.

Justine had explained the process of joining with a man, like some kind of unpleasant warning. There would be blood and pain. But God help her, why did she want to be hurt?

Justine had been wrong. It would be different with Fanworth than it had been for Justine. She had been forced into a liaison, with Mr Montague in this very shop.

'No!' She pushed him away, scrambling for safety. She had changed the look of the room, but she could not change the past. And at the thought of her poor, helpless sister, she wanted to be sick.

'No?' She could not look at him. But the frustration and anger were plain in his voice. 'You agreed.'

'Not here,' she said, breathing deeply until her stomach settled. Then she gave a hasty swipe at the tears on her cheeks. When she looked up at him, her gaze was every bit as unwavering as it had been when she'd bargained away her honour.

'It cannot be here. I cannot explain it to you. I will abide by our agreement. Anywhere but here.'

He pulled himself to a sitting position and stared at her. At the feel of his eyes on her body, she tugged the bodice of her gown up to cover breasts still wet from his kisses.

'Not here, then,' he said, without emotion.

The brief passion that had flashed between them was a pale imitation of the easy communion she thought they'd shared. It had been an illusion. He was as distant now as when he spoke to her sister. 'Tomorrow. In my rooms. And then, no running. No more excuses, or I will send for Mr Smith.'

She responded with a single nod.

He nodded back, as though he could no longer trust his voice. He stood, turning away from her and running a shaky hand through his chestnut hair. Then he was gone, the front door of the shop slamming behind him.

Chapter Five

'You are sure there will be no difficulty?' It was the third time Mr Pratchet had asked about the necklace that day.

For the third time, Margot answered with a quelling glance and a single word. 'None.'

'Perhaps it would be better if you allowed me...'

'No. I have spoken to Lord Fanworth. The matter is settled.' She ignored the leap her insides gave when she thought of the marquess. Pratchet had been right all along. It had all been nothing more than an elaborate seduction.

She would give Fanworth what he had wanted from the first. But she had done her best to minimise the damage through smart negotiation. If such a man was capable of keeping his word, then the matter would be settled in no time. She would not have to go to Justine about the necklace, or admit what had almost happened in the private salon.

But, for now, she had to endure Pratchet's curiosity. And if that was not bad enough, she was watched by the marquess as well. He'd passed by the shop in the early afternoon and glanced though the window at her, pausing just long enough to tip his hat and give her an ironic smile.

She had not been able to breathe until she was sure he was gone from view.

Thank God, he had agreed to leave when she'd begged him to on the previous evening. Once he had touched her, things had all happened too fast to understand. But the longer she had to think, the angrier she became. She was angry that he could pretend to blame her for the theft of the necklace. Angry that he had the nerve to be angry with her. And most angry of all that he had been so false to her for so long, acting as though he loved her and pretending that they shared some secret bond.

The least he could have done was stated his desires honestly, from the first. To make her believe that he cared for anything but her body had been unfair. If he had come to her some evening, after any one of those conversations, and suggested something they might do that would make that bond even deeper? She might have been seduced by smiles and soft words, opened her arms and gone freely. Instead, he had used blackmail. And though it disgusted her to admit it, the price was surprisingly low.

If last night had been an indication, the act of physical intimacy would not be as unpleasant as her sister had described. When he had come into the shop to claim her, Fanworth had been frightening, infuriating and intimidating. But at no point had he been repellent.

And while some might say he was threatening her with a fate worse than death, those people had never contemplated an earned place in a hangman's noose. Nor had they considered the other alternative: months or years wasting away in prison.

She could avoid punishment, if she went to her sister for help. But that would likely end with Justine insisting that she close the shop to prevent further such problems. If that happened, she would lose all she had sought to build. She would be encouraged to move in with Justine and Will, to live off their charity until such time as she made a proper marriage.

If she valued her independence, a few nights in the bed of a rich and handsome nobleman was hardly suffering. And if that man touched her as if she was made of porcelain and kissed like a fallen angel...

Apparently, when it came to the physical act of love, the pleasure varied with the participants. Though Justine sometimes blanched at the unpleasant memories of the jewellery shop, she was all smiles when she spoke of her husband.

She had shamelessly enjoyed the beginning of their first encounter. Perhaps, if she could manage to think of Stephen Standish while making love to Fanworth, it would be even better. But she had no intention of waiting meekly for him to take her. If she had her way, he would never be allowed over the threshold again. It had taken nearly a year to exorcise the demons from these rooms. Whether the result of her bargain with the marquess was good or bad, memories of it would not be allowed to taint the place where she meant to spend the rest of her life.

Tonight, she would go to him. She would be the aggressor, not the victim. It would set the tone for their blessedly brief relationship and allow her to escape with her dignity, even if she could not keep her virtue. She would like or dislike the act, as fancy took her. But she would perform it the four promised times. Then she would return here, never to think of it again.

She waited until the last customer had gone, shooed the clerks and shop girls out and gave Mr Pratchet another stern look to discourage his lingering. Then she took only a moment to straighten her hair before putting on a bonnet and shawl and exiting from the back of the shop into the street.

She did not want to be seen or questioned about this solitary journey. There was still enough light left in the sky to be easily seen and a woman walking alone on the Circus gave entirely the wrong impression.

Or perhaps it was the right one. She was most definitely up to no good. Her stomach twisted at the idea of going brazenly to the front door of the marquess's residence and demanding admittance. The fashionable street on which he lived was all too public and still full of holiday visitors on their way to various nightly balls and entertainments.

She stopped a street short of the building she knew to contain his residence, searching for the mews or alley that would lead her to the kitchens and the servants' entrance. Then she tipped the bonnet forward to shield her face, trying to disappear behind the scrap of veil that decorated its brim.

She counted down the row of doors until she came to the correct one and knocked quietly on the panel.

A scullery maid opened for her, wiping her wet hands against her apron.

For a moment, Margot's voice faltered. Then she whispered, 'Lord Fanworth?'

'If you have business with him, then go 'round the front,' the girl said, her suspicious glance sweeping Margot from head to toe.

'It's a private matter,' Margot said, even more quietly, glancing over her shoulder at the other servants working in the room. 'If you could show me how to get to his bedchamber…'

The girl let out a hiss of disapproval and held up a finger, indicating that she stay where she was. Then she turned from the door and went across the room to a woman sitting at one of the long wooden tables in the kitchen. Judging by the severe cut of her gown, and her equally severe expression, it was the housekeeper. There was a whispered conversation between the two and many sharp and disapproving glances cast in her direction.

Before a reason could be found to put her off, Margot stepped into the kitchen and shut the door behind her. Then she walked forward into the room to speak to the housekeeper directly. The woman did not rise as she approached, but watched her in silence.

'I have come to see Lord Fanworth,' she said, meeting the woman's gaze without flinching. 'He expects me.'

'Then it is surprising he is not here to greet you,' the woman responded, with a sour smile.

'If I could wait for him…'

'In his bedchamber,' the woman finished. By the look in her eyes, it was clear that she knew exactly why Margot had come. And she did not approve.

Margot could not blame her. She was not proud of her own actions, either. But pride and approval were not necessary. All that mattered was that she fulfil her part of the bargain so her life might return to normal.

She squared her shoulders and stared the woman down. 'Yes. I wish to wait for him in his bedchamber. No doubt he told you he would have a guest this evening. Unless you do not know what goes on in the house you manage.'

The woman opened her mouth as if to retort, then snapped it shut again. Without a word, she led the way to the servants' stairs and they climbed to the first floor in silence. The housekeeper opened the door and pointed down the hall. 'The third door is his suite of rooms. If the valet is there, it is up to you to explain yourself. I will not help you further.' Then she disappeared.

Margot swallowed the response that help was not necessary. If she did not want to appear helpless, then why was she shaking in her shoes? She took a moment to steady her knees and her nerves. Then she walked briskly down to the indicated door, opened it, entered and shut it behind her.

She stood in a pleasant but unremarkable sitting room. It certainly did not seem like the stronghold of an evil seducer. It looked more suitable to the man she thought she'd known.

It was also blissfully empty, as was the dressing room that connected to it and the bedroom that connected to that. As with the sitting room, there was nothing about the place Fanworth slept that made her think of a seraglio. It was rather a relief. If lying with him turned out to be unpleasant, she would rather it be devoid of erotic nonsense that would make her feel more awkward than she did already.

There was no sign of him as yet. But it would be better to be prepared for his arrival. With a sigh, she pulled off her shawl and bonnet and slipped out of her shoes, wiggling her toes in the thick rug before undoing her gown and pulling it over her head. She draped it over a chair beside the bed and removed petticoat, stays, shift and stockings, folding her clothing and piling it neatly on the seat.

She stood for a moment, naked at his bedside. She felt both free and rather ridiculous, standing about in her skin and making no move to dress. As an afterthought, she picked up the man's dressing gown spread at the end of the bed and slipped into it, knotting the sash loosely at her waist. She was more than covered now, lost in yards of silk. The sleeves fell to cover her hands and the hem trailed inches past her feet, pooling on floor around her.

It smelled of him. Because she could stop herself, she inhaled deeply and felt her knees go watery again. She wrapped her arms around her body to steady herself, but this only served to press the fabric of the gown against her bare skin and remind her of his arms the previous night. She sat down on the edge of the bed, suddenly dizzy. If he did not come soon, she would lose her nerve, dress and leave.

But it was already too late to escape. There was a commotion somewhere in the house. Slamming, shouting, and stomping about on the lower floor.

Was he always like this when at home? It certainly seemed in keeping with the sort of man who would go to such lengths to trick a humble shopkeeper out of her innocence.

She heard him shouting to a servant, as he approached his rooms. 'I d-d-d-do not need your help. You cannot g-g-get me anything I need, unless you can haul a certain woman to j-j-justice by her p-p-pretty guh-g-gold hair. I will call for Smith tomorrow and p-p-p-p...' The stutter ended in a clear exclamation of 'Bloody hell!' and a deep breath. 'God's teeth. I will bring the law down upon her. I...'

He stood in the doorway between the dressing room and the bedroom, tearing at his own cravat as a worried valet danced at his side, trying to catch the abused linen.

'You are here,' he said, frozen to the spot. The shouting was gone, replaced by quiet and confusion.

'As I promised, last night,' she said.

'I went to the shop,' he said.

That explained his anger. He thought she had gone back on their bargain. He was staring at her now, puzzlement clear in his eyes. But he did not speak, probably because asking how she had found his residence would result in another bout of stuttering.

She spared him. 'I knew your direction from before. When I realised who you were, I enquired after it.' She had made it a point to learn everything she could about the Marquess of Fanworth. Such curiosity was unladylike and all too embarrassing.

'Oh.' He was staring at her, obviously mollified, but still struggling with her sudden appearance in his rooms.

To remind him of the reason for it, she glanced in the direction of the valet and down at the dressing gown she wore.

He glanced at the valet as well and uttered a single word, 'Out.'

'Yes, my lord.' The servant evaporated with nothing more than a soft click of the sitting-room door.

Fanworth continued to stare at her, then said, 'Have you taken supper?'

'I am not hungry,' she said, sure that so much

as a bite would make her ill. Then, before she could lose her nerve, she stood, untied the sash and dropped the gown to the floor.

He continued to stare. At first, there was no change in his expression at all. Then, very deliberately, he looked into her eyes and gave a final tug on his cravat, letting it flutter to the floor. There was another pause, lasting several seconds, before he began to undo the buttons of his waistcoat.

Was it her imagination, or did his fingers tremble, just a little? Perhaps a more experienced woman would have helped him with his garments. It would have at least hurried the process of disrobing. He seemed to be taking unnecessary time with it.

The part of her that wanted this over as soon as possible warred with the part of her that wanted to grab her own clothes, turn and run before things progressed any further.

But if she was honest, there was a small portion of her soul loyal to neither of those sides. This one was fascinated by the deliberate pace he took and the patch of skin that had appeared at his neck, as he'd removed the neckcloth. As her eyes followed his hands down the line of undone buttons, she got occasional glimpses of bare chest through the gap in his shirt front.

He slipped coat and waistcoat off in one motion and hung them over the back of the chair that held her dress. Then he stripped his shirt over his head and tossed it carelessly in the direction of the wardrobe.

She swallowed, performing an unwilling inventory. He looked rather like one of the Townley marbles at the British Museum. But those had been frozen in place. Back, shoulders, arms, chest and stomach were all more beautiful when seen in motion. He turned away from her for a moment as he bent to remove his boots and hose, and she could not help but imagine him rising up with a discus in his hand, like a Greek athlete brought to life.

But there was more to be seen. In a few moments, he would be as naked as she was. Now he turned to face her and she found herself holding her breath, as the breeches fell.

At the proper boarding school her sister had forced her to attend, there had been a teacher who had actually been to Italy, and to France, before the war. It had been that woman's job to educate them in art and to train them to make even poorer copies of the sad sketches she had done of the art she had seen in the museums on her tour. That woman's well-thumbed sketchbook had contained a rather large collection of male nudes.

Had that poor woman been trying to minimise the male organ, to prevent shock to her students? Or was the marquess in some way deformed? He made Michelangelo's David look quite puny.

With barely a glance, the very real Adonis in front of her walked to his bed, threw back the covers and reclined. Then he patted the mattress at his side.

They were playing a game. She was quite sure of it. Her plan had been to startle him with her presence and her nakedness. His had been to come for her, to win her with kisses and touches, tricking her into last night's eager response.

In the end, that might have been easier. Now, he was daring her to prove her bravery and make the next move. Since she had set the tone for the evening, he meant to test her nerve.

Very well, then. Standing by the bed, gaping at him was accomplishing nothing. Though her feet seemed to be rooted to the floor, she would be here all night if she could not bring herself to move. She took three very deliberate steps towards the mattress, then knelt upon it. And then, with one deep breath, she swung a leg over the glorious male torso in front of her and straddled him.

From Justine's rather blunt explanation of biology, a good portion of it was an autonomic process. Once begun, it did not require thinking. And soon after that, it would be over. But how to get to that state? Clearly, one part did not leap to meet the other like a spawning trout. Fanworth lay beneath her, his arms folded behind his head and a sly smile upon his lips, enjoying her discomfort.

She closed her eyes and reached out and held the organ in front of her, which seemed even larger with proximity. For a moment, she lost her nerve again. Smooth. Or was it ridged? Soft. No, hard. Could a thing be both? What she was feeling was full of interesting contradictions. It was growing slippery. She tilted it towards her own body, tipping her hips trying to discover some way that two could become one.

'Stop.'

She froze, looking up at him. Fanworth was staring at her with a most odd expression. 'Am I hurting you?'

'No,' he admitted with a sigh. 'You are more likely to hurt yourself. Let me.' He reached forward, detached her grip and pulled her down to lay on top of him. Then he stroked her hair and kissed her. First, lightly, on the side of the head. His tongue traced her an ear, nuzzling her jaw line.

Her breathing was shallow, shaky. 'I do not need this. Just finish.'

'No,' he said softly and found her lips.

It was like it had been in the shop, when she had felt her reserve slip, and her will leave her. Only this time, it was better.

No, worse.

No. Better. Their mouths were sealed together, sharing life and breath. And while he might find speech difficult, his tongue was more than clever enough for kissing. He licked. He thrust. He teased. She would give him anything he asked, just for another kiss like this.

Her breasts were touching his chest. It felt good. Now, his hands were touching them, and it felt amazing. It was even better than it had been last night, when the gown had been in the way. Now she was free of her clothing, he could do whatever he liked to her. First he stroked, with just a fingertip. But then he pinched. The rougher he was with her, the more she wanted his touch. After a few moments of play, she slid up his body.

Slid.

She was growing wet, as he had. Her body was melting, longing to be one with him. She slid up his body and rested on her elbows, thrusting her bosom towards his mouth until he realised what she wanted and took the nipples, one after the other, between his lips, circling them with his tongue.

It was glorious.

And positioned thus, a most intimate part of her body was resting on top of his. He had been right. It had been too soon, before. Now, it was as if her body wanted to open like a mouth and swallow him whole. Yes. His hand had found the spot. Fingers inside her. Stretching. Good. But not enough. More. She wanted more. She needed more. And then, his hands were on her bottom, and…

It hurt. Why did it have to hurt? And why, even though it hurt, did she still want more? His hand was back between them again, touching somewhere close to where they joined. He was moving in her, groaning. Had he called her name? The sound was distant, as if he'd shouted into a storm. A few gentle, soothing strokes of his thumb had struck the core of her body like lightning. She shook, trembling not with cold but with heat. And he did as well, inside her, in a wet shuddering release.

It was over. And to her surprise, she wanted to remain in his arms, still joined to him, holding the moment for ever, hoping that the future might never come.

Chapter Six

Three.

It was the first thought in his head, on waking. And decidedly odd. It could not have been the chiming of the clock, for it was full daylight. He was quite sure he'd heard ten bells.

Then he remembered the night before and threw an arm to his side, searching for the body that should be lying next to his. He was alone in bed and the fine linen sheets were cold. He had fallen into an exhausted sleep after their love making, not so much from strenuous activity as the release of a month's eager anticipation, in one orgasmic rush.

As he'd drifted away, he'd imagined a lazy morning tempting her with morsels from his own breakfast plate and a bath scented with rose and lavender to ease any aches she had from the previous evening. He would scrub her back, rub her shoulders and comb out her hair. Perhaps she would end wrapped in his dressing gown, as he had discovered her the night before.

Apparently, she'd had no such plans. She had escaped while he'd slept. He could see the smear of blood on the bed beside him, a source of pride and anguish. No matter what sins she might be guilty of, she had not deceived him about her innocence.

Of course, that innocence was gone now. He had taken it.

Three.

He had promised her four nights only. One of those was already spent. If their first encounter was indicative of the rest, he had been a fool to agree to her bargain. Three was not nearly enough.

When he had not found her waiting penitent in her closed shop, he had been positive she'd betrayed him. He had been thinking in anger, wishing to punish. And then, she had been there, waiting for him, trying to turn the tables and control a situation she had not the least experience with.

It was shock enough to see her, in full naked glory, without any kind of preparation. The anger in him had evaporated, leaving the awe he'd felt when he'd first looked in her shop window and seen her smiling back at him. And when she had sat upon him and taken him in her inexpert hands…

What had he been thinking to suggest this at all?

But he had not been the one to suggest it. He might have implied, of course. She was the one who had made the offer of her body and set the boundaries of their association. It was he who was being tortured over this. He was to be given a taste of heaven and then yanked viciously back to earth in three more nights.

Assuming she allowed him that. She was a thief and not to be trusted. She had likely used the same skills that got her the necklace to creep past his defences and conceal herself in his own room. But that had not mattered, once they had gone to bed.

It was even less important, this morning. The theft of the rubies was settled to his satisfaction. He had the necklace back again and the setting. The money spent on the replacement was back in his bank. He had found the culprit and she was far too pretty to be turned over to the rough hands of justice. To send her to the gallows would have been like smashing a priceless artwork.

But he would not go so far as to forgive her for making a fool of him. If was probably for the best that she had overreached herself by selling him the rubies. Otherwise, he might have married her and ruined the rest of his life. Now, she would be what she should have been from the first: a temporary amusement.

Three times more.

Or longer, if he wished it. Why did he need to honour the agreement that he'd made to such a person?

He sighed. Because he was a gentleman. He had given his word. How stupid had that been? He would lose her long before he had tired of her, unless he could convince her to extend the arrangement. Until he discovered what he might offer to convince her, he must be miserly with the time he was promised.

He leapt from the bed and hurried naked to the writing desk to scribble a note. Then he rang for a footman.

Thank you for a delightful evening.

Since you left so soon after, you are likely fatigued. Wait a week's time before coming again, that we might renew our acquaintance when you are fully recovered.

Yours,

Fanworth

Damn him.

Margot crumpled the note, then noted the alarmed but curious look from the nearest shop girl and smoothed it again, folded it and tucked it into her bodice. It burned against her skin like a shameful kiss.

Yours, indeed. He was not hers, and she wouldn't have wanted him if he was. He did not like her. He did not trust her. He had tricked her into his bed. Now he meant to draw the agreement out.

She had hoped to be free and clear of him, with

her peace of mind returned, in less than a week. With too much time to brood on what had already occurred between them, she might never have a calm thought again. She glanced into the mirror kept on the counter, so that customers might admire the wares that they modelled. Did she look as changed as she felt?

She was tired, of course. She had left his room before the sun was fully up, taking the servants' stairs, as she had when she'd arrived. From there, it was home to wash, grab a few hours' sleep and be back downstairs in time to open the shop for the first customers.

She was hungry as well. She had missed supper, being too nervous to eat. Breakfast had been a hurried affair of cold tea and toast. Now she was coveting the Bath bun that Jasper was munching in the back room.

And she ached in strange places.

She yawned and caught another surprised glance from the girl polishing the class of the showcase.

Could she see something more than just fatigue? Worse yet, did Mr Pratchet suspect? Today, he kept looking at her with a vaguely disappointed glare, as though he had any right to concern himself over what she did after the shop closed.

Suppose that worldly poise she had admired in her older sister was actually the result of knowledge? The same light shining in the eyes of Eve as she had held out the apple to her husband.

She'd have preferred age-old wisdom to this feeling of smug satisfaction and the irrational desire to smile for no reason. She could not shake the feeling that there was something about her behaviour that signalled to the people around her what she had done.

Perhaps Fanworth was right. She would not have been able to stand another night like the previous one. If the first morning left her smiling, the next might make her laugh. By the fourth time, she would greet the dawn crowing like a rooster.

Oh, no, she would not. She shook her head to reinforce the thought, drawing a surprised look from the girl at the opposite counter. If she took to nodding and talking to herself, the employees would think she'd gone mad.

But that would be better than if they suspected

the truth. She had lost her innocence. It was a disaster, not a cause for celebration. It was a good thing she had no desire to marry, for what man would want her now?

There was one, of course. Nothing about last night, made her think that Fanworth's desire was abating. And even after learning his true character, she still wanted him, as well. Lord Fanworth was most decidedly not the man of her dreams. But he still had the face and body of her beloved Mr Standish. He might have tricked her into his bed, but once there his touch had been as sweet and gentle as she'd dreamt it would be.

The girl next to her was staring again and Margot frowned at her, then gave her a quick scold to send her across the room to dust the rings and polish the bracelets.

Her effort to contain herself came not a moment too soon. As soon as she was gone, Pratchet took the girls' place. He leaned towards her, far too close to be proper, so that he might speak in a whisper. 'I know what you have done.'

'I beg your pardon.' She managed the proper level of confused outrage, but was sure it was spoiled by the crimson flush that must be spilling across her hot cheeks.

He went on, as though she had confirmed his suspicions with a full confession. 'I warned you, from the first, that the Marquess of Fanworth was a dangerous man. Now he has confirmed it with his actions.'

'A receiver of stolen goods has no right to speak to me of honour,' she said, hoping that it did not sound too much like a confession. 'If you no longer like the working conditions here, I suggest you take your things and leave.'

'And abandon you in the busiest season, with so much unfinished work on the bench?' He glanced back towards his table which was heaped with orders. 'It is almost as unwise for you to threaten me as it was to become involved with the marquess.'

His recriminations were almost as annoying as the amount of truth in them. She would have been better off had she never met Lord Fanworth. Not any happier, certainly. But her life would be far less complicated. She gave Pratchet a pointed stare. 'While I know that you are capable of mending a broken watch, I have yet to see you successfully turn back time. Without that particular skill, what good can further conversation on the subject do either of us?'

He cleared his throat and straightened as though it were possible to present himself in a more impressive way. 'I come to you as a friend, Miss de Bryun. I am not trying to censure you, no matter how it might sound. I understand and sympathise. Although you have run this shop successfully, it was inevitable that you would be bound by the limitations of your gender. The same qualities which are the virtues of the female sex, your softness and sweet nature, make you easily led.'

'Do they, now?' she said, in a tone that should have given him warning, had he known her as well as he claimed to.

'You have fallen into the clutches of a devious and evil man. When it goes wrong, as it most assuredly will, you must come to me.'

'And exactly what will you do to help?' She tried to imagine Pratchet facing her seducer on the field of honour, only to be cut down like the weed he was.

'I could give an unexpected child my name,' he

said, glancing around to be sure that no one was near enough to hear. 'You and your family are far too well known in Bath to pretend that there was a legitimate marriage and a husband lost to sea or war.'

She had not thought of this. There must be ways to prevent pregnancy, or her sister would have fallen into that unfortunate state long before she had found a husband. But who did she dare ask about them?

Mr Pratchet continued to stare at her with an earnest, fatherly expression. 'You mock me. You think me old and foolish. I know you do. But surely a hasty marriage to a man who will care for you would be better than facing the disgrace of mothering a bastard.'

And here they were, back to her losing control of her own life to a man who knew what was best for her. When it had happened with Fanworth, at least there had been some pleasure gained in her mistake. But to enter into an empty marriage with a man she barely respected, for the sake of her reputation, was a punishment she did not deserve.

She turned to him then, giving him her most

firm, professional smile. 'We have already discussed the matter of marriage and I have no intention of entering into that state with you or anyone
else. As for the rest of it?' She gave a vague wave
of her hand meant to encompass her loss of innocence and any child that might have resulted
from her carelessness on the previous evening. 'I
have no idea what you are hinting at, Mr Pratchet.
And I do not wish to be enlightened. I fear you
are suggesting something that would be a grave
insult to my character. Now, as you say, there is
a considerable pile of work that you must attend
to. I suggest you apply yourself in the way you
were hired to do.'

The man gave her one last disapproving look,
before returning to his work station.

Margot closed her eyes for a moment, struggling to regain her calm. Even if it was already
too late, she was not yet ready to brood upon the
worst possible outcome of her current course of
action. She needed food and rest before she could
even consider what she would do if there was a
child. And if there was not, she must find a way
to take precautions in the future.

But it seemed she was to have no peace at all today. At the door were Justine and Daphne, doing up their parasols and smiling at her.

Margot smiled back, adjusting the position of the note in her bodice with a tug at the neckline of her gown.

Justine froze, staring back at her in shock. Her big sister knew her too well. With a single glance, she had uncovered every last secret. Then she relaxed, choosing to pretend that she had not. Her manner was all blissful ignorance as she said, 'Tea, Sister? Or have you no time for us today?'

'There is always time.' Margot gestured to the private salon. 'I am most unexpectedly hungry and could eat a plate of Sally Lunns all by myself.'

'I see,' Justine said. And now Daphne was looking at her with the same, overly curious expression.

'Or not,' Margot amended, trying to decide what was so shocking about wanting a bun with her tea. 'They would not be good for me, after all.'

'Indulging one's sweet tooth never is,' Daphne said. 'It leads to a thickening waist.'

Justine glared at her with such vehemence that

Daphne took a large bit of the first bun offered, giving her reason to remain silent.

Justine glanced around her again. 'No visit from the marquess this morning?'

'No,' Margot said, relieved to be able to answer truthfully. 'He has not been to the shop in almost a week.' Not in daylight, at least. She tried not to think about what they had been doing, on this very spot, two nights ago.

Justine gave an audible sigh of relief. 'That is good to know. You might have considered him a friend, love. But the true motives of such a man are often hard to predict. There is a rumour that he has taken up some new scandalous affair...'

'Really?' Margot said, taking a very deliberate sip of her tea. 'What concern is that of ours?'

'Simply that I would not want you to be hurt by his actions. Since you are fond of him—'

'Not really,' Margot inserted.

'That is good,' her sister said, doubtfully, setting aside her cup and reaching out to touch her sister's hand. 'Because there is no guarantee as to the permanence of his affections towards you or anyone else.'

Margot took another sip of tea. Any illusions she'd had about his motives had died with the discovery of the necklace. Strange how long ago that seemed and how little it seemed to matter. 'Do not worry about me, dear. I shall be fine. And I most assuredly will not allow myself to be hurt by the Marquess of Fanworth.'

Justine allowed herself to be comforted by the words. And then the three of them chatted of ordinary things for nearly an hour, before the two guests rose to leave.

Margot escorted them as far as the front door, only to see them step into the path of a gentleman walking by the shop. He was near enough so Margot could hear the polite greeting, 'Ladies', which was accompanied by a bow and a gesture permitting them to pass.

And through the glass of the shop window, she saw the shocked look on her sister's face as the Marquess of Fanworth looked into the shop directly at her and gave her a knowing smile.

Chapter Seven

With a week to prepare for it, Stephen took special care to set the scene for their next tryst. There was a dinner ready in the main dining room, should she wish to sup with him. If not, there was a selection of dainties arranged in the sitting room of his bedchamber. Oysters, prawns, strawberries and chilled champagne.

Perhaps it was too obvious that he had chosen foods that might inflame desire. Or perhaps not. She had known little enough about the act a week ago. Still, if there was a simple way to increase her ardour to the point where she might forget their ridiculous agreement and remain with him, he was not above resorting to it. He had no intention of letting her escape him after only three more nights. But such a strong-willed woman would wish to think the decision to stay had been hers.

He had sent her another note, earlier in the day, reminding her of their engagement and informing her that there would be a carriage waiting for her when the shop closed that would take her directly to his door with curtains drawn for her privacy. She might still refuse and find her own way here, but he would not be so stupid as to leave his bed-chamber to search for her, only to be surprised on his return. This time, he would claim the bat-tleground for his own.

For a moment, he considered greeting her as she had him, wearing nothing but his dressing gown. He rejected it, almost immediately. She would likely think it was vulgar. And he would feel more than a little ridiculous lounging about his rooms nearly naked. Instead, he took the time to change into his best tailored, dark coat and trimmed the lapel with a gold stickpin he had purchased in her shop.

Then he had nothing to do but to wait. When, at last, he heard the sound of the footman escort-ing her down the hall, he did his best to gain control of what could only be described as boyish enthusiasm.

That emotion was the parlance of Stephen Standish, the besotted fool who had fallen under the spell of the bewitching Margot de Bryun. The Marquess of Fanworth knew better. It was he who turned to face the door with a cool smile, as his lady entered.

Once again, he faltered.

He had not seen her in a week, other than brief glimpses through the shop window. No matter what he had promised, he could not manage to stay totally away from her. He savoured those walks along the street, pretending that he took them for his health. But if that was true, he must admit that a brief glimpse of her each day had become as necessary to his well-being as respiration.

The glass of the front window and blinding whiteness of the shop's interior must have dulled his perception, for he had noticed nothing unusual as he had glanced in at her. Could one week really so alter a person?

To say she was pale was an understatement. Her

normally luminous skin was as grey as moonstone and there were dark circles under her eyes. If he were to guess, he would say she had not slept since she'd dozed in his arms almost a week before. Her perfect brow was creased with worry. He had never seen her timid, but her step tonight was hesitant. She reminded him of one of the true invalids that came to take waters, hoping for miracle cure.

'Sit.' He came forward to her, taking her arm and leading her to a chair in the sitting room.

She resisted. 'I would prefer that we finish what I have come for.'

'And I would...' *Prefer.* He could feel the P tremble in his throat, 'I would rather we sit.' He poured the wine for her, wrapping her fingers around the stem of the glass.

She downed it in one swallow. Then she looked over the rim of the glass. 'Satisfied? May we begin, now?'

He refilled her glass. 'No.' He pushed the tray of oysters towards her.

She glanced down at them and shuddered. 'They

are out of season. I will likely end even more ill than I am already.'

'Ill?'

She gave him a wan smile and drank the second glass of wine. 'Yes. Perhaps it is the prospect of lying with you that makes me so.'

'The first time is always…' *painful, difficult* '…awkward. Tonight will be…' *different, better* '…more enjoyable.'

She laughed. 'For you, perhaps. But tomorrow, I will still be surrounded by people who know exactly what I have done and split their time between scolding me and worrying over me. I've had a week of that, while you grinned in the shop window at me like a dog at the butcher's shop.'

'Who knows?' Damn them all. He had promised discretion.

'My sister. Her friend. The rumours of your new lover were all about town before I'd even climbed from your bed. My employees guessed, just by looking at me. But they, at least, are too afraid to comment on it. Except for Mr Pratchet.'

'He can be damned.' Some words came easier than others and the curse flew unhindered. When he had visited the shop, he had seen Pratchet watching her just as she accused him of doing, as though she was the juiciest chop on the platter.

She gave Stephen a false smile and held out her glass for more champagne. 'You should not say such things about the man who is likely to be the father of your natural son.'

'I b-beg your p-p-pardon?' The suggestion shocked him out of his sang-froid.

'He has promised to marry me, should a pregnancy result from my indiscretions. For all I know, I am pregnant now. I feel like death warmed over.'

'You are simply overwrought,' he said. But if she was not? A mixture of terror and elation ran through him at the prospect that she might be carrying his child.

'Perhaps I am,' she said, then sprawled on the couch before him, almost spilling what wine was left in her glass. 'Or perhaps it will happen tonight, when you take me. And then I will end by marrying Pratchet to salvage my reputation and give the child a name.'

'That is nonsense,' he said, without a second thought. 'I would…'

'You would what?' she said with a bitter laugh. 'Give me money? I have more than enough to raise a bastard, I assure you.' She laughed again. 'You must have realised that yourself. I assume that is why you tricked me into dishonour, instead of making the simple monetary offer my friends and family warned me about.'

'I tricked you?' He had done no such thing. She had no right to act the innocent in this.

'Did you think Pratchet would keep your secret?' She gave a sorry shake of her head. 'He wants the shop for himself, you know. He was only too happy to buy the necklace when you brought it to him. In the end, he knew I would be the one to face the consequences.'

'When I sold the necklace...' he repeated. There was only one place she could have got such a ridiculous idea. Pratchet had misled her, probably hoping to leverage the lie into a quick marriage to a helpless, panicking female. It served the goldsmith right that the revelation had driven Margot straight into his bed. If he thought that Stephen would let her go again, he was sadly mistaken.

He looked at her, on the couch beside him, exhausted, but still beautiful. It was as if, for the first time in days, he could see her clearly. She was his beloved, not the conniving female his brother had...

Arthur.

It was all coming clear now. He had been tricked, right enough. And his offended honour had led him to punish an innocent.

She went on with her story, not noticing his silence. 'You could not have picked a better ally in Pratchet. How neatly the spoils are divided between you. You took my virtue and, when you are through with me, he will take my shop.' She reached for the bottle on her own this time, filling her glass to the brim and drinking deep. 'I thought you were my friend. Or, perhaps, something more than that.'

'I was. I am.' He reached out to stroke her hair.

She gave no indication she had heard his words. But instinctively, she leaned into the pressure of his palm, as though seeking comfort. 'Everyone warned me. They told me that you were dangerous and wanted to bed me. But I refused to believe.'

'They were right.' Though he could not have helped himself, it had been careless of him to love her. The world had assumed the worst.

'Then you needn't have bothered with trickery,' she said, in a small, hopeless voice. 'You were so handsome, so charming.' She let out a shaking breath, half-sigh, half-sob. 'There was no reason to steal the rubies or to threaten my business. If you needed money, I'd have given it to you. And if you wanted me, you had but to ask.'

His hand tightened on her shoulder, hiding his feelings of elation in a caress. She'd loved him, just as he'd hoped. 'I want you,' he said softly.

'Then take me. Do what you wish with me, so I may go home and rest. For I am so tired.' The defiance he had seen in her a week ago was gone now. She was too exhausted to resist him.

Which meant she was also too weak to accept. He removed his hand from her shoulder and stood. 'Eat.'

'I told you I could not.'

'I have no wish to make love to a corpse.' He pushed the tray to her, turning it so she might reach quail eggs, strawberries and cream. 'If you wish something else, then ring.'

She gave him a militant look.

He glared back at her to hide his smile. 'When you are through?' He pointed at the bed. 'Wait for me there.'

'And where will you be?'

'Out,' he said. There were things he needed to think about and the thought of Margot de Bryun in his bed left him deliciously unclear. If he was not firm in his resolve, he would be back with her, before he had done anything to earn a place at her side. He walked quickly to the door and through, shutting and locking it behind him.

The next morning, despite an uneasy night spent on the couch of his sitting room, the Marquess of Fanworth was nearly as resplendent as he had been while waiting to greet his lover. When he had returned to his rooms an hour after ejecting himself, Margot lay huddled under the covers, asleep in the middle of his great, soft bed. She looked tiny and helpless, curled in upon herself as a protection against God knew what indignity.

How could he have thought this innocent child was a devious jewel thief, entrapping him with her feminine wiles? Not a child at all, even if she looked like one in sleep. Her clothing was piled neatly on a chair, as it had been on their last evening together. He tried not to think of the naked flesh beneath the sheet, as he examined the empty wine bottle and the few bites of food missing from the tray. She would have a foul head in the morning, but at least she would sleep uninterrupted. If her colour was not better after some rest, he would call for a physician.

And it seemed exhaustion had been her problem. When he left the house at eight, she was still sleeping.

Stephen didn't bother calling for a carriage. There were times when it was better to walk. The exercise cleared his head, though it did not lessen his anger one bit. When he arrived at de Bryun's, his hand hit the door hard, causing it to spring open and bang against the wall. The little bell at the top that usually tinkled, lett out a rattling clank at the assault.

The shop girls and clerks looked up, alarmed at his entrance, but none had the nerve to approach him. It was strange to go to her shop, knowing full well that she was not there to meet him. But better that the world assume he did not know where she was than that she was asleep in his bed.

He went to the nearest clerk, a gawky boy with red hair and ears like jug handles, and favoured him with his most terrifying frown. 'Where is she?'

The boy was quaking in his shoes, but did not desert his post. 'Miss de Bryun is not here, my lord.' No attempt at pretending he was not titled, then. Had his ruse really been so thin as to be transparent?

He glared towards the back room and gave a dismissive gesture. 'Then...' Pratchet was nearly as hard to say as de Bryun. 'What's his name...?' He snapped his fingers, as if trying to remember.

The polite thing to do would have been to excuse himself and get the man. But in the absence of his mistress, the ginger clerk had reached the end of his nerve. 'Mr Pratchet!' The call came not as an answer, but a plaintive, rabbit's bleat for mercy.

The goldsmith appeared in the curtained doorway. His annoyance disappeared when he realised the reason for the disturbance. At the sight of the marquess, his face went a shade of white that rivalled the walls. 'Lord Fanworth.'

Stephen contained his glee at finding someone so obviously at fault and so worthy of his anger. He redoubled his glare, raised a finger, dire as death, and spoke the single word. 'You.'

As Stephen advanced, Pratchet shrank back, out of his reach, until they had passed through the doorway and were standing in the middle of the workroom. There would be privacy, in theory, at least. If half the shop clerks were not listening in at the doorway, he would be most disappointed in their lack of curiosity.

He backed Pratchet up until his arse hit the edge of his work table, sending a shower of loose gold chain-links scattering on the floor.

'I can explain, my lord.'

Stephen stared down at the man who had caused him to ruin his own future. 'Really?' He let his frown deepen, staring with even more intensity at the little man before him.

'When I was given the rubies, I did not know they were yours.'

'Liar.' Stephen swept an arm across the desk beside him, spilling its contents on the floor and tipping over the spirit lamp that Pratchet had been using to melt casting wax.

The goldsmith rushed to douse the flame, beating it out with the wool mat he had been working on, looking up frantically at Stephen. 'All right. I knew they were the Larchmont rubies. But I was too afraid to refuse.'

'You told her they came from me,' he said and watched the man squirm beneath his wrath.

'Not in so many words,' he argued. 'Is it my fault if she misunderstood?'

'It was your intention, all along.' Stephen continued to stare. When, at last, he spoke, he did so slowly and deliberately. It guaranteed the clarity of his consonants and had the added advantage of making each word sound as if it was to be the last thing Pratchet might hear. 'Who. Was. It?'

'Lord Arthur!' he blurted the expected answer, backing away from the table. 'Your brother brought them here. Who was I to refuse them? I went to the day's receipts and gave him everything we had. Then I hid the stones in the safe and made the transaction disappear.'

'You lied to her.'

'I did not. I said your family could not be trusted. I said I was frightened for her,' the man said, gathering what nerve he could, and spilling a torrent of words. 'It is clearly the truth. Your own actions prove that you do not care for her. Nor does she understand her place. She is getting above herself by running the shop at all. She needs the aid of a strong husband to protect and advise her, or it will all end in ruin.'

He had thought such a thing himself, two weeks ago. But he'd not been thinking of Pratchet as a font of wisdom.

'Aid from you?' He snorted. 'For your help, she might have been hanged as a thief.'

'You would not have let it come to that,' Pratchet said, still sounding surprisingly confident. 'If she was dead, you'd not have got what you truly wanted from her.'

That had been true, of course. But he had never considered that their affair would leave her vulnerable to a loveless marriage with this worm. 'So you spread rumours about her?'

'Her sister deserved to know the truth.' The man raised his chin, as if Margot's humiliation had been a righteous act and not despicable.

But it proved that what she'd said last night was true. All around her had known of their bargain and berated her with it until she could neither eat nor sleep. This man deserved whipping. Or at least he would have, if so much of what had happened had not been the result of Stephen's own unchecked pride.

But some punishment was definitely in order and it must suit the criminal. Stephen smiled. 'Since you are fond of truth telling, my agent, Smith, must hear some as well. I will explain that Margot is not at fault. It was you.'

'You would not dare,' Pratchet said, ruffling his feathers like a cockerel who did not know he was a capon. 'Your brother is equally guilty.'

'My brother is Larchmont's son. And you?' He snapped his fingers. 'Are no one.' Then he smiled with satisfaction at the thought of Pratchet squirming on the dock. It would likely not come to that. The man would run like a rabbit the moment he turned his back. But he would be seeking employment without reference and lie down at night in fear that the law might take him before dawn.

It was very similar to the ruined reputation and perpetual fear he had sought for Margot. In Stephen's mind, it seemed quite appropriate. He turned and walked away, to show that the interview was at an end, calling over his shoulder, 'Until we meet again, Mr...Ratchet.'

As he left the room, he heard the beginning of correction. But the goldsmith got as far as 'Pra...' before he realised that if the powerful, and likely vengeful Fanworth could not remember his name, it was probably for the best.

He turned back to give the man a final glare and exited the shop with a slam of the door that was almost as violent as his entrance had been.

Arthur had rooms in a hotel on the Circus. It was there that Stephen went next. He entered as he had at the jewellery shop, with much noise and no words. He pushed past the valet, going directly to where Arthur sat, nursing his usual morning hangover. Then, he grabbed his brother by the lapels and lifted him out of the chair, until his feet dangled, barely touching the floor. 'Explain.'

Arthur laughed with much more confidence than Pratchet had been able to manage. 'I suppose this is about the rubies.'

'You suppose?' Stephen punctuated the words with a little shake.

Arthur did his best, in his constrained position, to shrug. 'I needed money. Gambling debts, old boy. I could hardly ask his Grace. And I knew Mother would cry if she was forced to defend me, yet again. Better that she weep for her lost necklace than for her useless son.'

'You could have come to me,' Stephen reminded him. It would not have been the first time that he'd needed to rescue his younger brother from his own folly.

'Perhaps I should have,' Arthur admitted. 'Poor little Pratchet did not pay nearly so much as I'd hoped to get.'

'Then why take them there?'

'Two birds, Fanworth.' Arthur smiled. 'I was not the only one who needed rescuing. You were far too involved with the de Bryun woman. Something had to be done, before Larchmont got wind. I knew if Mother's rubies turned up missing, sooner or later, you would go to her, seeking a replacement.'

'Really.' Arthur had approved of the idea when Stephen had suggested it. Since his younger brother's judgement was notoriously bad, he should have seen it as an ill omen.

'I thought you'd recognise the stones from the first. But you had them reset, ready to give back to Mother.' Arthur laughed again. 'It really is rather amusing, when you think about it.'

'It. Is. Not.'

'But it has given you a reason to put Margot de Bryun in her proper place, on her back and in your bed. I assume, after a week with her, your lust-addled mind is clearing and you are no longer talking nonsense about making her a member of the family.'

At this, Stephen released his brother's coat, letting him drop to the floor. It was a relief to see Arthur waver on his feet, for a moment, then remain standing. What Stephen intended would hardly have been sporting had he collapsed.

He punched his brother, once, hard enough to break his aristocratic nose, and turned and left. It proved, yet again, that one did not need words, when one had actions.

Chapter Eight

When Margot finally woke, it was to daylight streaming through the curtains of the room and an aching head. There had been wine. Too much wine. And too little food, although it was not as if he hadn't offered.

Fanworth.

She sat up, gathering the covers about her for modesty. She was alone in the room save for a breakfast tray, set for one, and growing cold beside the bed.

She glanced around again to be absolutely sure that there was no servant lurking about, ready to help her. Then she climbed out of bed to get her clothes, grabbing a piece of burned toast as she did so. She did not remember lying with him on the previous evening. But then, she did not remember much of anything, other than the wine. Had he truly left her untouched? And if so, why? Perhaps she had done something to render herself repellent to him. Dear lord, she hoped she had not been sick. That would be even more embarrassing than waking naked in a strange bed.

But his disgust and her humiliation might be the easiest way out of the situation. If he had already tired of her, she could go home and sin no more, and pretend that none of this had ever happened. Assuming, of course, that he did not call down the law upon her because of the necklace.

But what should have been a relief left her vaguely sad. Was what he had felt for her really so shallow that it could be satisfied in a single night? It put paid to the fantasies she'd had that her dear Mr Standish would confess his title and his love, and offer some deep and lasting connection.

She'd have had to refuse, of course. Such a match would have been unworkable for both of them. But still, she could live a lifetime alone, sustained on an offer and perhaps a few chaste kisses...

Passionate kisses, she corrected, rewriting the

fantasy to include experience. Or perhaps the thing that had actually occurred between them. To have been loved once and well, as he had done the previous week, would be a bittersweet memory to balance a lifetime as a spinster. It would have been even better if he had been the honourable man she had fallen in love with and not a base villain who must be laughing at her naïveté.

She dressed hurriedly and downed the chocolate that had gone cold in the pot waiting for her to wake. The wine-induced headache eased somewhat with the food and a splash of cold water from the basin. Now, she must rush to the shop, for the clock on the mantel showed half past ten. Her arrival in yesterday's gown would be a fresh embarrassment. It was far too late to sneak back to her rooms before the business opened for the day. But the sleep had done her good. In spite of the humiliation, she was better rested than at any time since she'd discovered the truth about the rubies.

She reached the door to the hall, only to find it locked. She cursed once, softly, in French, then she rang for a servant. And rang again when the footman who came refused to allow her to pass without the master's permission.

The second summons brought the same housekeeper she had met on her first visit. Mrs Sims stared at her with a knowing glance that informed her she was no better than she should be, if she was on the wrong side of a man's door in the middle of the morning. A single, disapproving nod added that it was exactly what she has suspected would happen when Margot had turned up on the kitchen doorstep. After this protracted, silent judgement, she said, 'Lord Fanworth told me nothing about what to do with you, miss, other than to feed you. Which I did.'

'Thank you for that,' Margot said, attempting a friendly smile that had no effect on the scowling servant. 'It was delicious.'

By the surprised look on the housekeeper's face, Margot suspected that the tray had been served cold as a message from the kitchen.

'Now that breakfast is over, I must be going,' she said, giving another encouraging smile.

'Lord Fanworth said nothing about that, miss,' said Mrs Sims, not moving from the doorway.

Though she had wished to bar entrance on the first visit, for the second, Mrs Sims meant to guard the exit.

'Is Lord Fanworth in the habit of imprisoning women in his bedchambers against their will?' She'd meant it to sound sarcastic. But given the circumstances, it was a legitimate question.

The footman and the housekeeper looked at each other for a moment, trying to decide if an answer was expected. Then Mrs Sims said, 'It will take some time before the carriage can be prepared.'

'Then I shall walk,' Margot announced and pushed past them into the hall.

'I will summon a maid to accompany you,' Mrs Simms said with a sigh that implied that would take almost as long as the carriage. Clearly, she was stalling until Lord Fanworth could return.

'A maid will not be necessary,' Margot said and headed towards the servants' stairs.

The housekeeper cleaned her throat. 'The door is this way, miss.' Apparently paying the wages of sin involved exiting through the front door in broad daylight.

'Very well, then.' Margot straightened her bonnet and walked, head held high, down the stairs, out the front door and into the street. Her willingness to walk alone probably cemented her impropriety in the eyes of the housekeeper. But in Margot's opinion, it would be worse to be seen with a member of Fanworth's staff than to walk alone. She had no wish to add to the rumours already spreading about her improper relationship with the marquess.

Once she was on her way, she walked quickly to discourage conversation, should she meet someone she knew. If someone saw her walking on the wrong side of the street and noticed her attire was not immaculately starched perfection, there was little that could be said in argument.

Once she arrived at the building that housed her shop, she had hoped to slip up the side stairs to her rooms, largely unnoticed. It should have been easy for the main salon was already crowded with customers.

But at the first sight of her, Jasper seized her hand and pulled her to the back room. 'Miss de

Bryun, we were terribly worried about you. You were not here to unlock the door. And so much has occurred...'

'Calm yourself.' She detached his hand from her arm and glanced around the room. 'Where is Mr Pratchet? He should be helping in the main room, with the shop as busy as this.'

'That is the problem, miss. Mr Pratchet is gone.'

For a moment, all she felt was relief. Then she remembered the trouble it was likely to cause. 'Where did he go?' she said, puzzled. It was too early for a trip to the bank. And she could think of no other reason he might leave his post.

'We have no idea,' Jasper said. 'He did not say. But I do not think he is coming back. After the marquess spoke to him, he took his tools and—'

'The marquess was here?' she said, both surprised and annoyed. 'What did he want?'

Jasper looked even more nervous at this. 'He did not say, either. He asked after you, of course.'

'Or course,' she said drily.

'When he was told you were not here, he went into the workroom and spoke to Mr Pratchet, in private.'

'Do not pretend that none of you was eavesdropping,' she said in frustration. She had told the staff never to gossip about clients. But it would be most annoying if they took this instance, above all others, to follow a rule that they broke with regularity.

'He barely spoke,' Jasper admitted. 'And when he did, it was too quiet to hear. But he seemed angry. He nearly set the workbench on fire. The minute he left, Mr Pratchet gathered his tools and fled.'

What had she said the previous evening, to bring about such a visit? Perhaps it had been her mention of the man's offer that had set him off. The marquess might have taken exception to it and decided to dispense with a rival. It was madness. Was he really so possessive as to allow her no male friends? She had not really intended to wed Pratchet. Nothing short of total catastrophe would convince her to marry a man who was so shamelessly scheming for her hand.

Perhaps he was angry that Pratchet had revealed his part in the deception. If so, she was not sure she minded that he had faced the wrath of the marquess. Why should all the punishment for this situation fall on her shoulders? The loss of a gold-smith would be an inconvenience. But she'd have fired him herself, eventually, just to stop the pro-posals. The more she thought of it, the better she felt that he was gone.

'I think I understand what has happened,' she said, with a sigh. 'You are right. We will not be seeing Mr Pratchet again. Which means we are without a goldsmith.' She pinched the bridge of her nose, trying to focus her thoughts. 'We will manage as best we can, today. If someone comes, seeking repairs, we will send them to Mr Fair-weather in Bristol. Tomorrow, I shall put the ad back in the London papers to replace Mr Pratchet.'

'Very good, miss.'

'I will check the workbench to see what he has done. Hopefully, Mrs Harkness will not come for her necklace. I did not think he had finished mending it yesterday.'

Jasper looked nervous for a moment. 'Miss Ross dealt with that this morning, miss.'

'Did she now?' Margot glanced around the

room to see the youngest of the shop girls peering at her from the back room.

With a twitch of her skirt and a bowed head, Miss Ross stepped forward. 'It was only a single weak link, Miss de Bryun. And I have watched Mr Pratchet work, when the shop was not busy. A twist of the pliers, boric acid to prevent discolouration, a bit of flux, a bit of polish…' She gave another curtsy. 'I was very careful not to heat the rest of the chain.'

'It sounds as if you learned well,' Margot said, doubtfully. 'But I would still have preferred that you had waited until I returned, so I could see the finished work before it left the shop.'

'I sized a ring, as well,' the girl said shyly. 'It is still here.'

'Show it me.' Margot felt a strange thrill, half-apprehension, half-excitement. Could the recurring problem of overreaching goldsmiths be solved as easily as this?

The girl retreated into the back and returned with a plain gold band. 'It was only half a size,' she said modestly. 'And up is easier than down.

But really, down is nothing more than fixing a very big chain link.'

Margot took the ring and slipped it on to the sizing tool, noting the perfect roundness and the tidy way it rested, just on the size that the client had wished. Then she took up a jeweller's loupe, examining each fraction of the curve for imperfection or weakness. When she looked up again, she smiled. 'You do nice work, Miss Ross. Very tidy. I am sure, if this is a sample, that the chain was fine as well. Are there other repairs that you feel capable of attempting?'

They brought out the list and examined each item. The girl felt confident with all but two of the current requests.

'Perhaps we can find something similar in the shop that you might use to practise those skills,' Margot suggested. 'We could break an existing piece and let you mend it.'

'Ruin good work?' the girl said, shocked.

'They are my pieces. There is no reason we cannot do as we wish with them,' Margot said reasonably. 'If it means that I do not have to place an ad for goldsmith, it is worth the risk.' Even better if it meant that she would not have to put up with the inconvenience of a gentleman developing a penchant for her, or her shop.

'From now on, I wish you to spend as much time as possible at the workbench, attempting these repairs in order of difficulty. If that goes well, we can discuss wax casting.'

The girl's eyes lit up. 'I watched him at that, as well. He sometimes let me work the little bellows and pour moulds. It would be ever so exciting.'

'Very good, then.' Margot thought for a moment. 'And it is hardly fair for me to employ you at the rate of a junior clerk if you are taking on more work. As of this moment, you will see a rise in salary to reflect your new duties.'

The girl's eyes were as round as the ring in her hand. 'Thank you, miss.'

She felt a ripple of jealousy throughout the room. It was hardly warranted. Other than Jasper, her staff had done little more than gossip and panic. 'As for the rest,' she said, loud enough to be heard, 'we must see how we do without Mr Pratchet to help with the customers. It is quite possible that there might be more for all, if one less person is employed here.'

There was an awed whispering amongst the other clerks. And for the first time in a week it was not about Miss de Bryun's recent strange behaviour.

All went well, for the rest of the day, except for one incident.

The shop was near to closing and the room quiet. The two well-dressed ladies who were her final customers had refused her help more than once. Yet they continued to glance in her direction as they pretended to stare down into a case of diamond ear bobs.

Margot moved closer to them, hoping that they would be encouraged to either make a purchase or leave. It was near to eight o'clock and despite the good night's sleep she'd got, she was eager to return to her own rooms.

Before they realised she was near, she caught two dire words of their whispered conversation.

'Fanworth's mistress.'

Chapter Nine

'A gentleman to see you, my lord.'

Stephen looked up from the writing desk in his private sitting room and waited for the footman to explain himself.

'Lord William Felkirk,' the man supplied.

'I will be there shortly.' He had been expecting such a visit since the last time he'd seen Margot de Bryun.

She deserved an apology, of course. Once she had forgiven him, he could make the offer he'd intended from the first. She'd been an innocent dupe in the matter of the necklace and would never have been involved at all, had he not taken an interest in her. That had been the thing to draw his brother's negative attention. Then, Stephen had made everything worse by jumping to conclusions. But how could he ever set things right if she refused to so much as look him in the eye?

Conversation had been so easy between them, just a fortnight ago. She'd looked up and smiled each time he passed by the shop, as if she'd been searching each face that passed by her window, hoping to see him. In turn, he had been able to talk for hours without having to plot out each sentence to avoid embarrassment.

Now, when he paused each day in his walk past her shop, she gave him a Medusa stare, as if she would strike him dead should he cross the threshold. In response, his tongue felt like leather in his mouth. Even if he could have managed speech, when they had their agreement, he had given his word not to return to the shop. He could not very well hold private words of apology up on a card from the other side of the front window.

It was some consolation to see that when she was angry, her colour was slightly improved. But he missed the carefree happiness that had drawn him to her in the first place. He must find a way to return it to her, if only to put things back the way he'd found them before he had entered her shop and ruined her life.

Since he could not manage to speak to her, he'd thought a letter might do. He attempted one on several occasions, his left hand smudging and crabbing the letters, forming them even worse than usual. Carefully phrased sentences, which spoke of 'mistakes' and 'misunderstandings' were feeble and inadequate for the situation at hand. After hours of painstaking composition, he'd managed a worthy attempt. He'd taken full responsibility for what had happened. He offered marriage if she would have it. At the very least, he would give her so much money that she might close the shop and move to a place where no one had ever heard of her, or her association with him.

It was returned unopened.

Apparently, she feared another request for a tryst and had decided that their association was at an end. He could not blame her. By now, even he had heard the rumours that the Marquess of Fanworth had taken up with the jeweller. When he entered an assembly room, pushed his way through a rout, or attended a musicale, ladies whispered about it and gentlemen congratulated him on his excellent taste.

He glared at all of them until they went silent. But as soon as he was out of earshot, the conversation began again. Avoiding her did not stop the gossip. But going to her would only make it worse.

Something must be done. This visit from Felkirk came as a relief. She might choose to shun Stephen. It was wise to do so, he had earned her scorn. But in her brother-in-law, Stephen would have an intermediary who could not be ignored.

'Felkirk,' he greeted the man with his most formal bow, silently thanking God that it had not been the Duke of Buh-Buh-Belston he'd needed to greet. The man come to deal with him was the duke's brother. In precedence, he was beneath Stephen and owed him respect. But his demeanour was of a disapproving schoolmaster, about to administer a whipping.

Felkirk took the chair he offered, but refused refreshment with a look that said he would rather sup from a pig's trough than share a drink with the person he'd come to visit. 'I understand that you have entered into a relationship with Miss Margot de Bryun?'

'If I had, I would not speak of it,' Stephen replied, narrowing his eyes to seem equally disapproving.

'The lady in question is my wife's sister.'

'I know.' When he'd imagined a union between them, he'd hung much on this relationship. The older sister had married well. If Margot was also elevated, would it really come as such a surprise?

'Our connection is not widely known,' Felkirk admitted. 'That has less to do with any reticence on the part of my family than it does with the single-minded independence of Miss de Bryun. Margot did not wish to trade on the family name to make her success.'

'She would not have to,' he replied with no hesitation. 'Her work is the finest I have seen in England.'

By the shocked look on Felkirk's face, a two-sentence reply from the notoriously silent Fanworth must have seemed like a flood of words. That it came in praise of a woman he refused to acknowledge was even more interesting.

Felkirk gave a brief nod. 'I will inform her sister of the fact. It will be a great comfort to her. But other matters are not.' He gave Stephen a searching look, allowing him to draw his own conclusions.

When Stephen did not immediately answer, Felkirk continued. 'My wife and her sister are very close. They are similar in appearance as well.'

'Then you are fortunate to have a married a lovely woman,' Stephen said, again surprising the man again with his honesty.

'I am aware of that. But I am also aware of the sort of attention such beauty can draw when one appears to be alone and unprotected—'

'Her looks are not Margot's only virtue,' Stephen interrupted, feeling suddenly eloquent when presented with his favourite subject. 'She is an intelligent young woman with an excellent sense of humour.'

If Felkirk had been surprised before, now he looked positively shocked by this quick admission. 'Since we can agree on her many excellent qualities, you must also understand how troubling it is to hear that she is entering into a liaison not likely to end in marriage.'

'I fail to see how it can end any other way,' Stephen said. Then he fixed Felkirk with a look that implied he was the one to put a dishonourable intent on their rather unorthodox courtship.

'You mean to...' It was like watching air leak from a billowing sail. Felkirk had not been prepared to win so easily.

'Marry her,' Stephen finished.

Felkirk responded to this with stunned silence.

The man expected him to explain himself. Not bloody likely, since any attempt to describe the current circumstances would end in a stammering mess. Stephen continued to stare, waiting for the man to speak.

He saw Felkirk's eyes narrowing again, as he tried to decide what to make of this sudden and complete victory. 'Margot would not tell us the reason that she went to you.'

'Nor will I,' Stephen replied and continued to stare at him.

'A marriage is necessary, of course, and the sooner the better. The rumours flow faster than the water at the pump room.' Felkirk stated the obvious, but in a doubtful tone as though suddenly unsure of his mission.

'A special licence then. I will set off for London immediately.'

'Immediately,' Felkirk repeated. 'Without speaking to the lady you are to marry?'

Stephen sighed. Perhaps, with some other girl, the matter could be easily settled between gentlemen. But his Margot was not the sort to let her future be decided by others. 'I suppose I shall have to.'

'You do not wish to speak to her?' Felkirk was clearly offended.

'She will not speak to me,' Stephen clarified.

'Despite the circumstances, I will not force her to wed you, if she does not wish to,' Felkirk said.

'She wishes it,' Stephen said. 'She is not yet aware of the fact. But she wants to marry.'

'Then, how...?'

It was an excellent, if unfinished question. And then a plan occurred to him. 'You must offer her an urgent reason to wed,' Stephen said with a smile. 'For example, if there were threat of a...'

He took a deep breath and forced the word out. 'A duel…'

'You wish me to call you out over this?' Felkirk said with an incredulous snort.

'If you would be so kind,' Stephen said, relaxing.

'I had hoped it would not come to that.'

'It is not for my sake,' Stephen reminded him. 'It is for hers.'

'But suppose she wishes me to fight you?'

'If I know Margot,' Stephen said, surprised by his own confidence, 'she will not. She would think it foolish.' His Margot was far too sensible to demand that men fight for her honour.

'Then what good can it do?' Felkirk asked.

'Your wife will not take it so lightly. Suppose I am not the one injured?'

Felkirk gave him a speculative look. 'Think you can best me, do you?'

Actually, he did. Fencing had been an excellent way to channel the rage he felt at his impediment. Those who had seen him with a blade deemed him a master. But now, he shrugged. 'For the sake of argument, you must make her think I might.

Though it may appear so, Margot will not risk the happiness of her sister to see me suffer.' If such a strong-willed creature as his Margot had wanted to see him bleed, she'd want to stab him herself. Since he was as yet unmarked, he had hope.

Stephen favoured his future in-law with an expression that was positively benign. 'Surely, accepting my name and title is not too much of a hardship, if it assures your safety.'

Felkirk held up a hand, as if to stem the rising tide of confusing arguments. 'Am I to understand you? You are willing to marry my sister-in-law, if she would accept you?'

If he could not explain the whole story to Felkirk, he could at least give the man one small bit of truth. 'It would make me the happiest man in England to take Margot de Bryun as my wife.' He spoke slowly, to add clarity as well as gravitas. And he was relieved that there was not a tremor or a slur over the name of his beloved.

There was another significant pause before Felkirk said, 'Will your family say the same?'

In such moments, there was no point in giving

ground. 'I assume you mean Larchmont. If you ask the question, you know the answer.'

'Your father is notorious for his strong opinions,' Felkirk said, as diplomatically as possible.

'His opinions do not concern me,' Stephen replied. 'I would be more interested to know the opinion of your family. Since you are married to the woman's sister, I assume I will be welcome in your house. And your brother married a cit's daughter.'

'The circumstances in both cases were unusual,' Felkirk said, but did not elaborate.

'In this case, they are not. I wish to marry Margot for love. The rest is immaterial.'

'Other than her unwillingness to see or to speak to you, of course,' Felkirk added. 'Or to tell any of us what is the matter so that we might know whether we do greater harm than good by yoking her to a man she despises.'

She had loved him once. That he had managed to ruin that…

Idiot. Dullard.

And that was his father speaking again. He would stand squarely against such a marriage—

that was all the more reason to press onwards. 'I have no wish to make her unhappy by forcing this union. I simply wish for her to realise that she will be happy, should she marry me.'

'And to bring her to this realisation, you wish to trick her into accepting you?' Felkirk said with a frown.

It was not a trick, precisely. He merely wished to nudge her in the direction she secretly wished to go.

'The choice is still hers,' he said. But he knew her well enough to be predict her reaction. She would marry him. After they were together, he would find a way to make her believe that he had nothing to do with the necklace. Once she realised that they were both victims of a hoax, it would be as it had been and they would be happy.

For now, he smiled at Felkirk as though eager to meet his doom. 'At least, we will see, soon enough, if she cares whether I am living or dead.'

'But surely, you must see that this is best for all of us.' Justine was using the tone she had taken throughout their childhood to bring her difficult sister into line.

Margot gritted her teeth to resist responding. What she had hoped would be a quiet Sunday visit with her sister and brother-in-law was turning into a lecture on what she must do to salvage her reputation. Now that Margot was fully of age, Justine had no right to make such demands. Her life was her own. She could ruin it if she wished.

That was an especially petty argument and another reason to remain silent. She had not wanted ruin. But neither did she want to wed Fanworth.

Justine tried again. 'If he can be persuaded to behave honourably, we can end this quietly. Your good name will be restored and you will have married into one of the most respected families in England.'

'If I can be persuaded to take him, more like,' Margot said. She doubted she would have to make such a decision. If the plan hinged on Fanworth behaving honourably, there was no need to bother with it.

'If he can be made to offer, of course you will say yes.'

'Do you mean to answer for me, as well?' Justine had taken far too much on herself already. 'I did not ask you to send Will to him, angling after a proposal.'

'You did not have to ask,' Justine said. 'He did it for my sake.' She reached out to take her sister's hand. 'I cannot stand by to see you destroyed over this foolish shop, just as it very nearly destroyed me.'

'It was not the shop,' Margot argued. 'Mr Montague was at fault for what happened to you.'

'But if you had been here, to see the looks polite women gave me, as I walked down the street...' Justine's voice broke. 'I will not live to see the same thing happen to you. You will marry the marquess and retire to his home in Derbyshire. That is even further away than Wales. No one will know of the scandal and you might start anew.'

'And what would become of the business?' Margot said. Justine seemed to be ignoring the practicalities.

'We will close this place and never think about it again. It has brought nothing but bad luck to our family and we will do well to be rid of it.'

As always, Justine was blaming the building and its contents for any and all of their troubles over the last twenty years. It was nonsense, of course. But better that she fault the shop than take any part of the blame on herself, for things she had no control over.

'If only I had refused, when you told me of your plan of taking over de Bryun's,' Justine said, the first tear trickling down her cheek, 'I might have kept you safe.'

Now they were returning to Margot's least-favourite subject, the need for her older sister to control everything and make any and all sacrifices necessary to save the family. But it was unusual to see her so upset that she resorted to tears.

Gently but firmly, she withdrew her hand from Justine's, then returned it to cover her sister's hands to console her. 'You cannot fix everything, you know. You certainly cannot fix this, just by marrying me off to Fanworth and selling the shop. Especially since I am of age now and unwilling to do either of those things. I will stay away from him and be sure that he stays away from me. By next summer, all will be forgotten.'

Unless, of course, the marquess had her arrested for the theft of the Larchmont rubies. She must hope that the week's silence since their last meeting was a sign he deemed it better to forget certain details than to risk her blurting ugly truths about his character as part of a Newgate broadside.

Justine was readying her next argument when they heard the sound of footsteps in the hall and her husband appeared in the doorway. At the sight of his tearful wife, Will Felkirk gave Margot a grim, disapproving look, as if to blame her for Justine's distress. Then he came and sat at her side, close enough so their thighs touched and extricated her hands from Margot's so he might hold them himself.

His wife stared up at him with watery eyes. 'You have spoken to him?'

Will paused a moment, then glanced at Margot and nodded. 'The matter is settled.'

Margot breathed a sigh of relief. 'Good. The sooner we can all put this nonsense behind us, the better.'

'I put it to him quite simply. He will marry you, or I will meet him at dawn.'

'A duel?' At this, the normally stoic Justine dissolved into sobs.

'It will not come to that,' Margot insisted, alarmed at her sister's extreme reaction.

'You will marry him, then, if he offers?' Will said, clearly relieved.

'Not if he was the last man on earth,' she replied, not bothering to think.

'He is not the last man on earth. He is a marquess,' Justine snapped, tears still streaming down her face. 'Now stop acting like an honourable match with the son of a peer is a fate worse than death.'

'I cannot stand to be in the same room with him, ever again.'

'If you do not like him, you need not live with him after the ceremony. But you will not draw my husband into fighting him, to protect the reputation you were careless with.'

'I did not ask him to be involved in this,' Margot snapped back.

'And I did. Because I had no idea you would be such a ninny about it. It was quite clear, a few weeks ago, that you doted on the man. You would not leave him alone when I warned you what would happen. And now, because of your stubbornness, my Will could be injured, or even killed.'

'There, there,' Will said, gathering her close.

'It will not come to that,' Margot repeated. 'Do not allow yourself to become overwrought over nothing.'

'I will if I wish to,' Justine said, with another shower of tears. 'If you have no care for yourself, think of the child that will be born fatherless...'

This was too much. 'I am not increasing,' Margot insisted. She had been more than a little relieved to discover that herself.

'I was not talking about you. What about my child?' This was followed by more tears from Justine and a glare from Will.

'You?' Of course. It had to be true. Justine had been making sly admissions of morning illness, of tiredness, of a desire to start a family and of the readying of the nursery at the old Bellston manor. But had her shy sister ever said in so many words that a birth was imminent? Or had Margot been too busy with the shop, and with Fanworth, to notice?

'And now Will might have to risk himself because you are unwilling to listen to reason,' Justine said, sniffling into the handkerchief that her husband offered her.

He leaned close to her, whispering into her ear and kissing the side of her face. Whatever he had said seemed to calm her, for she turned back and pressed her face into his hair, smothering his lips with her own.

If possible, an awkward situation was becoming even worse. She had missed the obvious clues to her sister's pregnancy. Though she refused to believe that she had put him at risk of his life, she had managed to involve Will in her problems. And now they had all but forgotten she was here.

When Will managed to disengage his wife from himself, he looked over her head, glaring again at Margot. 'As you can see, Justine is distressed by recent events.'

'But I cannot simply marry him,' she said. Even when things had been going well, she had known that was impossible.

Now he was looking at her with disgust as though she were the most selfish creature on Earth. 'Either I will put the announcement of your betrothal in tomorrow's paper, or we will fight on Tuesday morning. One of us will be injured, or perhaps killed. I hope you are satisfied with that prospect, for there is no third alternative.'

At this, Justine let out a wail. 'There will be no fighting. I will go to him, myself, if that is needed. I will throw myself on my knees and beg him to do what is right for our family.' She raised a hand to her temple in a gesture that Margot would have called melodramatic, if her sister had ever been guilty of such a thing. 'Do not worry, Margot, I will take care of everything. Just as I always have.'

'No!' Margot's shout of frustration was every bit as loud and dramatic as the behaviour of the other two people in the room. But it brought an instantaneous halt to their emoting. 'I will go myself, immediately. And I will go alone. I will be back in time for supper, to tell you what we have decided.'

Whatever happened, it would not involve a

pregnant Justine, on her knees, begging Fanworth for anything. She might think that it was her job to sacrifice for all and for ever. But, by the Blessed Virgin, Margot had caused this problem and she would solve it herself with no help from her older sister.

Chapter Ten

For the third time in as many weeks, Margot was arriving unescorted at the house of the Marquess of Fanworth. This time, she gave up even pretending that it was possible to move unnoticed and greeted any acquaintances she passed with the cheery wave of an unrepentant harlot. Let them think what they would. She was fairly sure that, no matter what happened today, it would end in a story that would give the whole town something to gossip about. For all she cared, they could choke on their tongues.

Mrs Sims admitted her without a raised eyebrow. Then she glanced at the steps towards the bedrooms, as though expecting Margot intended to show herself up. The insult was subtle, but it was there, all the same.

For all she knew, this woman was the one who had set the town buzzing about her disgraceful behaviour and brought Justine and Will down upon her like hounds on a hare. If so, she had best hope that Margot was not about to become Lady Fanworth, for there would be hell to pay.

'I wish to speak to Lord Fanworth. In the drawing room, please. Or wherever it is he receives guests,' Margot said, offering an equally aloof expression.

The housekeeper let out a dismissive sniff to remind her that they both knew why she was not familiar with the proper, public rooms of my lord's apartments. Then she took Margot down a short hall to the salon, not bothering with an offer of refreshments before she shut the door.

A short time later it opened again, and Fanworth appeared. He did not bother to bow. 'Margot?' He greeted her with that strange, soft pronunciation that went right under her skin and made her shiver, even on a warm summer day. But it was not dread she felt. It was anticipation.

Damn him. Even as she knew the truth about him, she could not help wanting him more than a little. She did not bother answering. Suppose there was an unexpected softness in her own voice as she spoke his name in return? 'I have just been speaking with my sister and brother-in-law.'

'Lord William,' he responded with a nod.

'And I have been informed that I must either wring a proposal out of you, or it is pistols at dawn.'

He thought for a moment. 'Easy enough.' He went down on one knee. 'Would you do me the honour of accepting my offer of marriage?' He delivered the proposal with such unemotional precision that, for a moment, she did not even understand the words. Then, just for a moment, she thought she saw a twitch at the corner of his lip. Behind that frosty façade, he was laughing at her. So she laughed in response, aloud and without kindness.

He looked up at her in surprise. 'I amuse you?'

'Because you can't be serious,' she said, sure that it was so.

'I am,' he said, just as sombre. 'Unless you wish to see me fight Felkirk.'

'Of course I do not,' she said. 'We will explain

to William that there is no reason for that. What I did, I...I did of my own free will. It is over now. The less said about it, the better.'

'Technically, it is not,' he said, still sombre. 'We agreed on four. Once is not four.'

'Twice,' she said.

'Nothing happened that night,' he said. 'It is not fair of you to count it.'

'I have no idea what happened,' she replied. 'Because I was inebriated. You should know that. You were the one plying me with spirits.'

'Champagne is hardly a spirit.'

'Even worse. It is an aphrodisiac,' she argued.

'Not an effective one,' he countered. 'Nothing happened.'

'Then I am glad of it. I would rather go to gaol than to lay with you again,' she said in frustration. 'Look at the trouble a single time has caused me.'

'A marriage will stop the tattle. The rest...' He paused, as though he had suddenly lost his train of thought. Then he gave a helpless shrug. '...can be settled after the wedding.'

'But I do not want to marry you,' she said.

'Then I must fight Felkirk,' he said with a sigh and stood up, brushing the dust from the knees of his breaches.

'The devil you will,' she said, at the end of her patience. 'I will not risk you shooting my sister's husband because of me.' Or being shot himself. Though she loathed the man, she could raise no pleasure at the thought of him bleeding on the ground.

'It is a matter of honour. Such a challenge cannot be ignored.'

'Your honour, or mine?' she said. 'And what does William have to do with any of it?'

'B-B…' He took a breath. 'Yours and mine. Felkirk's as well. You are of his family…'

'A distant part, surely.'

'Near enough to matter.'

'Well, do not shoot him. I will give you whatever you want.'

'I was thinking swords,' he said, ignoring her offer. 'As the one who was challenged, I choose the weapon. There is an advantage to fighting with the left hand.' He gave an experimental lunge.

She tried not to notice his tight calves and the rippling of muscle beneath his coat.

'You bastard,' she said in a low breath.

'Unfortunately, I am legitimate,' he replied, rising and sheathing an imaginary sword.

'If you had not run Mr Pratchet off, I could have married him,' she said.

He looked surprised. 'You want him instead?'

'He was concerned for me.' And the shop, of course. That had been his real concern all along. But if she'd have married him, she'd have had to share his bed. Even now, the thought sent a chill through her. 'Marrying Mr Pratchet would have been the logical thing to do.'

'And you are a shining example of feminine logic,' said Fanworth, expressionless.

'I thought I had no choice.'

'You could have married me,' he suggested.

'You had not asked,' she reminded him.

'I have now. I await your answer.'

He was being sarcastic to goad her. She responded in kind. 'Why would you want to marry the thief who stole your mother's necklace? Is the punishment we agreed on no longer enough?'

'You did not take the necklace,' he said. 'I am sorry for having accused you.'

Now she had found the flaw in his logic. 'You knew that all along. Because you were the one to take it.'

'I am innocent as well.'

'You? Innocent? I cannot think of a less accurate word to describe you,'

He shrugged. 'In this case, it is accurate.'

'I do not believe you. It is but another lie. You have told many of those, since I met you, I cannot keep track of them.'

'Think as you will. Today I speak true.'

She sighed, wishing it were true. Then it might still be possible to trust him. 'It makes no difference now, whether you are lying or not. What's been done cannot be undone.'

'Then why not turn it to your advantage?'

'By marrying you?'

'Yes.'

It did not sound like help at all. It sounded like the world would think her a title hunter, instead of just a whore. 'I would be the only marchioness with a jewellery shop of her own,' she finished glumly.

'Eventually you would be a d-duchess,' he added, displaying more vulnerability than she had seen in ages.

'That would make it worse.'

Just for a moment, she saw another flicker of his old smile, as if the man she had always wanted was still there, hiding beneath the surface. Had this not been her fantasy, when he'd first visited the shop? That he would see past the difference in their different stations and want to wed her?

That had been nothing more than a dream. This was real, and nothing at all like she'd imagined. How could she explain to Justine that the reality was not what she wanted?

There were no words that would help. Her sister saw no further than her own miserable past and would be ecstatic at the prospect of such a marriage.

And the Marquess of Fanworth was still standing before her, awaiting her answer.

'What will your father say?' she said, grasping at straws.

His response was little more than the slightest

twitch of an eyelid and a brief statement. 'It does not signify.' He might not care. He was annoyed that she had asked. But the silence accompanying it spoke loud enough. His family would not like it.

She closed her eyes and pinched the bridge of her nose, praying that when she opened them again, she would see some other solution to the situation at hand. 'You are adamant, then. We marry, or you duel.'

'Yes.'

'And you are willing to marry me.'

'Yes.'

'Then the only thing preventing a resolution to your argument with Will...'

'To Felkirk's argument with me,' he corrected.

'The only thing preventing a resolution...' she repeated.

'Is you.' His response was so gentle that, with her eyes closed, she could swear it was Stephen Standish who had spoken.

But then she opened her eyes and saw the cool, aloof Marquess of Fanworth, staring back at her as though he could see the chair behind her. Of course he would marry her. It meant that she would be back in his bed without the inconvenience of clandestine meetings and gossiping staff.

He had tricked her. Again.

She glared at him. 'Very well, then. Since I have no choice in the matter, I will accept. Send word through Lord William when you have the licence and we will put an end to this nonsense. Until then, I do not wish to see you or speak to you, or receive notes, letters, gifts or anything else. And for God's sake, stop wandering past my shop, gaping in the windows at me. It is distracting to me and to my customers. And now, good day.'

It had not gone as he'd hoped.

Of course, Stephen had hoped, when down on his knees before the woman he loved, he'd have been able to come up with words a little more stirring than a brief proposal. At least he could have managed a better apology for his mistreatment of her.

I did not mean to dishonour you. I promised there would be no gossip. I did not give the necklace to Pratchet. It was my brother...

There were other ways to say those things, he was sure. But when he opened his mouth to tell her, his mind was awash with impossible consonants. And as it always did, his tongue glued itself to the roof of his mouth until he could say practically nothing.

Then he smiled. It had gone wrong. But all the same, she had agreed to wed him. He would get the licence, reserve the Abbey and make all things ready. Then, once they were properly joined in matrimony, he would take her back to his bed and demonstrate the sincerity of his affection in a physical way that did not become muddled when he most needed it to be clear.

When she had been properly loved and realised that he could buy her the contents of a dozen jewellery shops, she would see his side of things. There would be no more nonsense about the inconvenience of having a title. She would take her proper place in society. And all of London would take one look at her and fall at her dainty feet.

Once she realised that she was happy, she would smile at him again. He would be able to speak freely to her, just as he used to. They would declare their love. And their life together would be as he'd imagined it, from the first moment he'd met her. Perfection.

Chapter Eleven

'My lord, his Grace is waiting for you in the salon.' The butler in Fanworth's London town house announced the visitor with the barest trace of sympathy, for he knew of the strained relations between peer and heir. Stephen had hoped that his visit to the city to get a special licence would pass unnoticed. Obviously, this was not the case.

Usually, he made it a point to avoid any city where Larchmont was staying. The duke remained in London long past the point when fashionable people had quit it for summer. So of course, Stephen spent early summer in Bath. By the time Larchmont arrived to take the water and bathe his gout, Stephen would be on his way to Derbyshire again. If the duke came home for Christmas, Stephen went to London. So passed the year.

Because of his impending marriage, a temporary intersection of their schedules was inevitable.
But Stephen had hoped that it would be postponed
until after the ceremony when there was less the
duke could do to influence matters. Still, if it occurred now, his bride might be spared the meeting
with her father-in-law until the man had grown
used to the idea. 'Thank, you,' he answered to the
butler. Then he braced himself for battle as the
servant opened the door to the receiving room.

Larchmont had aged. But who had not? It had
been nearly five years since their last meeting.
His hair was more grey than brown and the lines
on his face had deepened. Five years ago, the
ebony walking stick he always carried had been
little more than a vanity. But as the door opened,
he was using it for support. When he realised
he had been caught in a show of weakness, the
duke straightened and twirled it in his hand as if
to prove that it had been nothing more than mo-
mentary fatigue.

Stephen did not bother with a greeting. He had
learned long ago that to speak was to open himself to ridicule. As a child, he'd had no choice in

the matter. But now that he was a grown man, he did not have to put up with it in his own house. He stood before the duke and offered a respectful, but silent bow.

His father dispensed with cordiality as well and went immediately to the matter at hand. 'I suppose you know why I am here.'

'No idea,' Stephen replied, with an insolent shrug.

'The word is all over London that you have gone to Doctors' Commons for a special licence. You mean to be married. To some shop girl in Bath.'

The temptation was there to offer correction about Margot's position. Shopkeeper would have been a more accurate term. Since it would not have changed his father's opinion, Stephen held his tongue.

'I forbid it.'

'I am of age,' Stephen said, without raising his tone.

'It does not matter. You should act in regard to my wishes, since you continue to spend the money I send you.'

How like his father, to bring up the stipend he

was awarded each month. The money was largely symbolic. He had long ago learned to invest his inheritance in such a way that a supplement was not needed. 'I will manage without,' he said.

'Do you mean to give back the house as well? You live quite comfortably on my estate in Derbyshire. Perhaps it would be better if I put it up for rent.'

It would be dashed inconvenient. Stephen had grown quite fond of that house and the properties around it. Though the income generated went into his father's pocket, he had been acting as landlord since his majority and considered it almost his own.

But he would relinquish it if he must. He chose the counter-attack most likely to madden his *pater familias*. 'Then I shall have to live off my wife's money. She owns her shop. It is quite successful.'

His father gave a growl, part-frustration, and part-anguish. 'No Standish has ever needed to marry for money.'

As far as Stephen could tell, none had married for love either. 'I shall be the first,' he said, answering both conditions.

'You bring shame upon our good name,' his father said, in disgust,

'So you always tell me,' Stephen replied.

'I should have drowned you like a puppy, the minute I realised you were foolish. Instead, I endured years of your squalling and yammering and stuh-stuh-stuttering. When I think of the heir I could have had…'

Which meant Arthur, he supposed. He was the son that Larchmont deserved: drunken, dishonest and disrespectful. But at least he had a silver tongue to talk his way out of the trouble he caused. 'It was not my request to be spawned by you. Nor to be first. Though I share your regret, I cannot change it.'

'But you could modify your behaviour,' the duke suggested. 'As you did your abominable penmanship.'

If he was not careful to wear gloves in summer, the sun still brought out the white scar across his knuckles that marked the reason Stephen had finally learned to use his right hand to make his letters. God knew what his father intended to break to improve his taste in women. 'I am satisfied with the way things are,' he said, with a calm that was sure to annoy Larchmont.

'Because you are an idiot. And like all idiots, you cannot control your lust. Tear up the licence, give this girl a bank draft and send her away. Then, perhaps we can find someone from a decent family who is thick-witted enough to have you.'

Stephen could think of a myriad of responses to this, involving his marks at Oxford, the shrewdness of his investments and the circumspection he employed when navigating the slew of marriage-minded young ladies who were more than willing to overlook his speech impediment for a chance to be the next Duchess of Larchmont. And then, of course, there was the genuine feeling he had for the woman his father wished him to cast off.

But as it always did, after a few minutes arguing with his father he could feel his tongue tiring. It was ready to slur or stick on even the simplest words, as it had done when he was a child. So he remained silent.

His father held a hand to his ear. 'What's that, boy? I did not hear your answer.'

So he gave the only one necessary. 'No.'

The old man glared at him in shock. 'I beg your pardon? I do not get your meaning.'

At this, Stephen laughed. 'And you call me idiot. Even I understand a word of one syllable.' It would feel good to say it again, so he did. 'No.'

'You seriously mean to defy me in this?' his father said, as always surprised that the world did not turn at his pleasure.

'Yes.' The fight was grinding to a halt, as it always did, when he had run out of words. Though the duke sometimes made up for the silence with one last, protracted rant, Stephen was down to monosyllables and weighty silence. He stared at the old man, barely blinking, with the same look of disdain he used on the rest of England. It was an expression that said that the person before him had nothing more of interest to contribute. The unfortunate presence would be borne with as little patience as was necessary, until the interloper withdrew.

The look was one of the least painful lessons he had received from his father. He had been on the receiving end of it since he'd said his first, malformed words. He had learned to ignore it. While a glare might frighten, it did not hurt nearly as much as a stout cane across the knuckles. But he had learned to use it as well. Now, he was every bit as skilled at hauteur as his father.

The duke was not impressed. 'Do not think to turn stubborn on me now. Call off this wedding or I will see that you and your bride are banned from society.'

What hardship would that be? he wondered. He had no use for society and Margot had not yet been introduced to the people who might snub her. 'As you will.' Then he continued to fix his father with the direct stare that informed him that the conversation was at an end.

The duke stared back at him, in a silent battle of wills.

This was a new tactic. It was doomed to failure, Stephen was sure. Silence was his oldest friend. He could remain wrapped in it indefinitely, quiet as a rock, still as an open grave. But Larchmont was an orator, an arguer, a speechifier. He could not *not* talk any more than he could hold his breath and wait to grow gills.

A minute passed. And then another. It was an

eye blink for Stephen and an eternity for his father. And then, the duke erupted in a stream of curses, elegant and un-repetitive. He damned his son, his shop girl, resulting children, grandchildren and great-grandchildren. He damned the whole Larchmont line from Stephen until the end of time and then, with a final shake of his cane, he turned and stormed off, trailing invective like a stable boot trailed muck, all the way down the hall and out into the street.

It was the middle of a workday and Margot was trapped, against her will, two roads down from Milsom Street. While the sign on the shop insisted, in delicate gold letters, that it was a *beau jour*, she found nothing particularly *beau* about it. She had a new goldsmith to train and shrinking receipts from a sudden lack of custom. She did not have time to shop.

She swatted at the hands of the seamstress, trying to coax her into yet another style fresh from London, and glared at her sister. 'I told you, this trip is unnecessary. I have gowns enough. Any of them will do.'

'You would wear an old gown to your wedding?' Justine looked at her in amazement. 'Surely that is bad luck.'

Fine words from a woman who had eloped to Scotland after several months of pretending marriage to the man she eventually wed. Justine had been too much in love to care what she wore to the brief ceremony. And Will Felkirk had been so bewitched, he'd have declared her radiant though she had been wrapped in a grain sack.

Of course, Lord Fanworth was not similarly blinded by love. Someone of his rank probably expected that she would dress for the nuptials. It made her want this even less. 'The situation is unlucky enough already. I doubt my choice of gown will make it worse.'

'Nonsense,' Justine said, turning her sister and unfastening the current unsatisfactory choice. She had all but dragged Margot by the hair to get her to the modiste's. Perhaps she sought to make up for her own lack of a wedding gown by choosing her sister's. 'You got on fine with Fanworth before. Whatever problems you are having now will pass as quickly as they've arisen.'

For a moment, Margot felt that fleeting hope as well. It had been so good, when they had just sat together and talked. Of course, that was before she had seen the man he really was. Now, they seemed to get on best when the lights were out and no talking was necessary. But what was she to do with him, when the sun was up? Were they destined for a lifetime of sitting across the breakfast table from each other in uncomfortable silence?

'At least I will not have to sit in his house, day in, day out, pretending that I am content. I will still have the shop.' Not really, of course. Once they married, it was his. But surely, he could allow her this one small thing, after casually disrupting her entire life.

'You are not planning on continuing with this.' Justine's expression was incredulous, as though the possibility had never occurred to her.

'Have I said anything, at any time, about a wish to give it up?' Surely she had sacrificed enough since meeting Fanworth. She had given him her innocence. She had tarnished her reputation. And now she was marrying him to keep the peace.

But she had no intention of moulding herself into a new person, just to gain approval from him or society. It was simply too much to ask.

Justine opened her mouth to argue, then smiled. 'That is something you must discuss with your husband, not with me. I am only here to find something suitable for a future marchioness to wear to her wedding.'

'Discuss it with Fanworth? What a ridiculous notion. Once he got what he wanted from me, he no longer had a reason to speak. If there is to be a discussion over my future, I will have both sides of it, while he stands in the corner and glares.'

Her frank admission that there had been something more than polite courting involved in the match caused the seamstress to drop her pins in shock. Then she scooped them up, slipped a few between her lips and pinched them shut in a tight, disapproving line.

And now, if she did not spend according to her new station, there would be more gossip. Margot sighed and pointed to several of the most expensive gowns in the catalogue and requested they be made in equally expensive fabrics.

Justine and the modiste gave mutual sighs of satisfaction, both convinced that they had won the battle of wills.

Perhaps they had. When she did not focus on the reason for the purchase, she was rather enjoying the attention. It had been ages since she'd spent time or money on herself. Since she could afford the purchase, what harm would it do her to look nice?

And she had to admit, if Justine was an indication of this woman's skill, this shop would be an excellent place to start. Her sister's gown was neither as gaudy as Mr Montague had encouraged, or as overly simple as she'd chosen for herself. Since she had married, Justine favoured styles that were well cut and elegant, often trimmed with the lace she made with her own hands.

Now that Margot looked at it, the frock they had all but forced her into was really quite charming. A bit of colour in her wardrobe would not be a bad thing. The pale blue of this silk suited her well, though it could have used some sort of ornament on the bodice.

As if she had guessed what Margot was thinking, Justine removed a small parcel from her reticule and set it on the counter in front of them. 'And you will do me the honour of wearing this as well,' she said. Then she unwrapped the tissue to reveal the most splendid lace fichu Margot had ever seen. 'I made it for your wedding day.'

'But when did you find the time?' There had to be many hours of work in the little triangle, for the threads that made up the knots were as fine as cobweb.

'I have been making things for you for years.' Justine gave an eager smile. 'Mother's old trunk is full of them.'

Margot did not like to think of the hundreds of hours her sister must have spent, preparing for a day that she had been doing her best to avoid. It was clear that Justine had pinned all her hopes on a favourable match for her little sister, ending in a proper, church wedding. Despite her misgivings, Margot owed it to her to at least attempt the part of happy bride.

It would be interesting to see Fanworth's reaction should she appear, for once, smartly turned out. He had only seen her dressed for work.

And naked, of course.

'Would the *mademoiselle* like a glass of lemonade? Or water, perhaps. She is quite flushed.'

'Thank you,' Margot said, trying to find an explanation for her sudden blush. 'The stays are just a bit too tight for me.'

'Of course.' The woman loosened the lacing and paused in the fitting to bring the promised refreshment.

Margot took a sip, but it did nothing to cool the heat as she thought of the marquess, gazing at her in surprise. Perhaps he would be moved to comment on how well she was looking. Even if he did not respond with the effusive compliments he had paid her in the past, it would be nice to see him smile again.

Or perhaps he would give her the same cold stare he had used lately, as though he could not quite remember what had moved him to speak in the first place.

She dragged her mind back to her sister, who had draped the lace around her shoulders and was tucking it into the neckline of the gown. Margot ran her finger along the picot edge of the scarf. 'It is too beautiful. With all the trouble I have caused, I am not worthy of such a gift.'

'You must accept it, for I have made you an entire trousseau,' Justine said, with a happy sigh. 'I cannot tell you what a relief it is that you are getting married. I have been planning for this day for as long as I can remember. When I had no hope for my own future, I dreamed of yours. And I made sure that you would have all the things I would not. It gave me hope.'

'Oh. Thank you.' Margot took another sip from the crystal glass of lemonade, which seemed overly sweet compared to the bitter taste in her mouth. She'd had only one wish for her own future: a successful jewellery shop where she could design and sell pretty things she had not even planned to wear for herself. That dream had come true, through her own hard work and stubbornness.

And through Justine's sacrifices, of course. She had been the one to endure the advances of the repellent Mr Montague while Margot had stayed safe at school, oblivious to what was happening. Even after she had learned the truth, she had been no help in rescuing Justine from her predicament. All that Justine asked in return was that she be happy.

And married.

'I am sure your current nightgowns are very sensible.' Her sister was still talking, Margot's lack of enthusiasm ignored. 'But I have made things for you, Margot. For your wedding night.' Justine gave a sly smile. 'Soft fabrics. Lace as delicate as a moth wing. You will look beautiful. And I am sure the marquess will find them very flattering.'

'The marquess,' Margot repeated. At least she knew what to expect from him, on their wedding night. Perhaps he was not the kind, friendly man who had visited her shop. But neither was he the odious Mr Montague, or pompous Mr Pratchet.

Fanworth was young, handsome and virile. Would a man like that find a lace nightrail flattering? Like the wolf in the fairy story, he would lick his lips and swallow her whole. And it was a shock to realise what a willing victim she would be. She could already imagine his hot breath on her skin.

Her sister pushed against her arm to wake her from the daydream. 'You are so busy thinking about your husband to be that you cannot see him right before your eyes. He is walking on the street, opposite.'

And so he was. She had not seen him since the curious day of his proposal. But then, she had not really expected to. Will had mentioned that he would be gone for at least a week, since he must go to London for the licence. When he had returned, he'd abided by her request for privacy, sending the date and time of the ceremony in a message to her brother-in-law.

If he were to break his vow and walk past her shop, this was his usual time to do so. But instead, he was several streets away and walking in the wrong direction. And he was not alone.

He walked arm in arm with a lady she had not seen before. She was a dark-haired beauty, nearly his equal in height, and moving with the grace and poise of the finest society ladies.

Stephen was absorbed in conversation with her, totally unaware that his future wife watched from a dress-shop window. But then, why would he expect her here, in the middle of a workday? She should be in her shop, nearly a quarter of a mile away from where he talked with this beautiful stranger.

The easy flow of his words was something she had not seen in weeks. While she watched, he tipped his head skyward and laughed out loud at something the woman said to him. It was not the usual behaviour of the Marquess of Fanworth, who had no time or desire to speak or be spoken to.

What she was witnessing today was annoyingly familiar. From her concealment, she watched Stephen Standish, at his most charming. And he was using that charm on his next conquest.

Chapter Twelve

Stephen was a nervous bridegroom.

That was all right, he supposed. According to the cliché, such nerves were expected. He had always assumed that they were in some way precoital.

He had no concerns in that matter. Even if they had not dispensed with the first intimacy some weeks ago, he had the utmost confidence in his abilities once the lights were out and the conversation was over.

But, the actual wedding required speaking, on cue and without hesitation. That was another matter entirely.

Since the moment he had been sure of her acceptance, he had got out the lectionary and begun to practise his part. The servants were used to the sound of him droning to himself before events such as this. On the rare times he had to speak in a crowd, he practised incessantly until the words came as second nature.

That a few short phrases should be so difficult was annoying. He supposed it was the gravity of the situation that caused the trouble. That such an important word should begin with a D made it all the worse.

And now, he was pacing in the nave, muttering softly to himself while awaiting the appearance of his bride. 'To love and to cherish, until d-d-duh…' He punched his fist into his twitching left hand. 'Damn it to hell!'

The curse echoed through the high ceiling of the Abbey, bringing a shocked gasp from the bishop.

Stephen smiled to put the man at ease, then went back to his practising. At least he would not have trouble with the bit at the beginning. He took a deep breath to relax and let the two words flow from his lips. 'I will.'

'You will what?'

He turned to see his bride, standing in the doorway with her sister and Felkirk. She had heard him practising. But the empathy that had drawn him to her on their first meeting was gone. Today, she was annoyed.

'Nothing,' he said hurriedly, glancing down at his watch as though obsessing over a prompt start to the ceremony.

'Fanworth?' Felkirk was at his side now, offering a frown of disapproval and a shallow bow. The man was still not sure whether his sympathies lay with the bride, the groom, or neither of the above.

'Felkirk.' Stephen bowed in response.

'Are we ready to begin?'

Stephen nodded.

Felkirk glanced about him and gave a nod of acknowledgement to the Coltons, who had accompanied his future wife and her sister. They were the only guests. 'I do not see your family here to witness the event.'

It was because Stephen had not bothered to inform them of the date. It would have been nice to see his mother again, so that she might meet the woman who would be the next duchess. But if Mother came, so would the duke. The interview with his father had been difficult enough without encouraging him to come and spoil the wedding.

And God forbid either of them brought Arthur. It would be a disaster.

He had told his sister, of course. She was the last person in the world he wished to offend. But she could not come alone. As a sop to Louisa, he had taken her to the jewellery shop, hoping that a violation of his promise to avoid his bride would be forgiven, so that he might make this very important introduction. But on that day, of all the days in the year, Miss de Bryun had elected to go shopping rather than man the counter of her shop.

Perhaps it was a sign that she might be ready to forgo the place in favour of married life. It would make things easier if she were just a bit more like other women of his acquaintance. Of course, none of those women had fascinated him in the way this one did.

At the moment, the object of his affections was having a whispered argument with her sister who was straightening the very attractive lace collar that adorned Margot's ordinary work frock.

'I thought we agreed, the blue was more be-coming.'

'And I told you that such purchases were not necessary. Your gift suits this just as well.'

'But it is so plain,' her sister was practically wailing at her.

'Hush.'

It was true, he supposed. She was hardly dressed for a wedding. But it was very similar to the dress she had been wearing the first time he'd seen her. That was a day worthy of commemoration. He saw no reason to complain.

The frown upon her face now did not bode well for their future. She swept a glance over the empty church, then back at him, accusing. 'Are we wait-ing for other guests?' It was clear from her ex-pression that she knew they were not. 'Or might we get this over with?'

He tried to smother his annoyance. Perhaps things had not gone as either of them had hoped. But was marrying into one of the noblest fami-lies in England really such a hardship?

Then he thought of his family and gave her credit for an accurate understanding of her future as a Standish. He signalled the bishop that they were ready to begin.

Once the ceremony was underway, he breathed a silent sigh of relief. There were not likely to be any objections from the bride's family, since they had arranged the match. The empty pews on his side would be peacefully silent. Margot was far too sensible to refuse, rather than say the vows. More importantly, she would never have gone to the trouble of leaving her shop just for the opportunity to embarrass him at the altar.

The success of the day was all on him. If he could manage to say the words, just as he practised them, there would be no trouble.

And then, the bishop began to read. 'Who can find a virtuous woman? Her price is far above rubies.' Why, of all topics, had he picked that one? He could not have chosen worse if he'd read all of Revelations. Stephen could feel the rage rolling from the woman at his side like a cloud of steam. She must think he'd suggested it as some sort of cruel joke. But now that they were in the midst of things, he could not demand that the officiant stop and chose a more suitable verse. He would find a way to make it up to her later. For now, they would have to brazen it out.

And then, things got worse.

The bishop began the vows. 'Do you, Stephen Xavier, take this woman...'

Do.

He had read the prayer book for hours, until he knew the entire ceremony by heart. Apparently, he knew it better than the bishop. The phrase was supposed to begin... 'Will you...?' And to that, he could answer effortlessly. But this sudden, unexpected move to the present tense made everything impossible.

He could answer, 'I will', just as he'd expected to. But would she think there was some doubt about his willingness of the moment? The more he thought about it, the harder it was to say anything at all.

The church was silent. The bishop had got to the end of his part and was waiting for an answer. It was his turn. He must say something, and say it immediately. 'Yes.'

For a moment, the bishop paused, as if about to correct him.

So Stephen chased the single word with a scowl of such ferocity that the man immediately turned to Margot and repeated her part.

At the end of it, she gave the same dramatic pause that he had done, while fumbling for his words. Then, very deliberately, she said, 'I do.'

The next few minutes were a nightmare. He staggered through the few sentences of his next speech, omitting some words, slurring others and making bizarre substitutions that turned sacred vows into nonsense.

The bishop watched in shocked silence. His soon-to-be wife stood frozen at his side. The back of his neck burned with the heat of Felkirk's angry gaze. There was no way to turn back the day like a clock and start it over again. So Stephen glared back at them all, daring them to challenge him out loud.

With one more slight hesitation, the bishop moved on to Margot's vows.

After a single, resigned sigh, she spoke them perfectly.

Now it was time for the rings. This would go better, he was sure. It sometimes helped when he could connect his statements to some solid object. He reached into his pocket and clutched the ring tightly in his palm, imagining the delicate ridges along the silver band and the amethyst set artfully between them.

She had designed it herself, at his request. He had asked her for a ring for the most beautiful lady in England. Then he had suggested that she use her personal taste as a guide, hoping she would understand his meaning.

When she had presented him with the finished project, she'd admitted that she was quite proud of it. Then she had assured him that there was not a female alive who wouldn't fall at his feet should he offer it. When he presented it to her, here, on this most important of days, she would understand that this marriage was no mistake. It had been his intention all along.

And then, she would forgive him for the mess he'd made of things. Most importantly, she would not notice if he worshipped with self and not body, and endowed her with things and not goods. 'Til death was the most important bit. He barked the words, almost like a curse. But he got it out, once and clearly, sending the 'us do part' rushing after it.

There. Finished.

He had been too busy to notice her reaction. Apparently, she had lied when she had extolled the virtues of her work. There was at least one woman breathing who was totally unimpressed by the ring. The woman who had made it was staring down at it with disbelief.

For a moment, he still hoped that her expression would change to the surprised smile he'd been expecting. Instead, he saw disappointment, disgust and anger. He could feel the faint pull as her hand tried to escape his grasp, twisting as though trying to gain release from something particularly unpleasant.

He held even tighter, until the struggling stopped. It was an instinctive response and it embarrassed him. He should not be holding the woman he had just promised to love and cherish like she was a prisoner on the way to the gallows.

But she had just promised to love him as well. It should not be necessary to detain her. None of this was as it should be. Nor was the cheek she offered him to kiss, before they turned to leave the silent sanctuary. They were married, just as he'd hoped it would be—yet it was all wrong.

Perhaps the worst was over. He had done his best to see that, despite the lack of guests, their marriage would be a festive occasion. For the wedding breakfast, he'd reserved the front parlour of the most fashionable hotel in Bath. The food was excellent. The fish melted on the tongue like butter. The ham was so thinly sliced as to be near transparent, but smoky and wonderful. The fruit bowls were heaped high with grapes, strawberries and oranges straight from Seville. He had chosen the wines himself, the most exclusive vintages from his own cellars. Even though the party was small, the cake towered above them, draped in real ivy and sugar roses.

Despite all this, Margot glanced impatiently about her and ate as if the food had no flavour at all.

'Is there somewhere else you wished to be?' he drawled, taking a sip of his wine. These words were clear and unhalting. Why was sarcasm was so much easier than normal speech?

'Yes,' she said, not bothering to elaborate.

Anywhere but here, he supposed.

'It is not as if there is any real reason for celebration,' she said. 'You are as trapped in this marriage as I.'

'For the sake of the others, we must smile and...' be polite...*gracious*... He gave up and shrugged, glancing in the direction of her sister.

'I do not see why,' she said, with almost masculine bluntness. 'They know the circumstances as well as we do.'

'Then for the strangers walking by on the street,' he said, with an expansive gesture that almost knocked over his wine glass.

'Because you had us seated near a front window on the most travelled street in town,' she said, obviously disgusted by his choice.

Because he was proud of his new wife and wanted to make it clear that their affair had been no casual flirtation with a woman of a lower class. He had fallen in love with Margot de Bryun and did not care who saw it. He shrugged again. 'Everyone loves a wedding.'

'Everyone,' she said. It was both a statement and a question.

'At least those who have never married,' he said, thinking of his own parents.

'But no one in your family, apparently,' she said. So she was thinking of them as well.

'This event is no concern of theirs.' At the last minute, he'd almost changed his mind on inviting Arthur. His brother owed Margot an apology. And the little sod deserved to see that his scheme, in the end, had come to nothing. If from spite alone, Stephen had forced circumstances around to the way he'd planned them to be.

It had been like trying to turn a barge with a birch twig. But, by God, it had been done.

'If we'd made our plans according to whom and whom did not have a legitimate stake in this union, we need not have done it at all,' she said. 'You had but to release me from my bargain with you and I could have returned to my shop as if nothing had happened.'

'Nothing?' he said. Was that what their love making had been to her, then?

'There was no harm done.' She took a hurried

sip of wine. 'Despite my fears, there is no child imminent. While there has been a negative impact upon the business from my notoriety, I am sure, by next summer, it will be forgotten. To the next crop of holiday goers, I would have been nothing more than a merchant.'

'That is all that matters to you, is it? Your shop?' A normal woman would have lamented for her lost honour.

'It is my only source of income and therefore a primary concern,' she said, using the masculine logic upon him again.

'That is no longer true,' he reminded her. 'You are married. The value of the shop pales in comparison to the rest of my holdings.'

'The rest...' There was an ominous pause as she considered his words. 'Because it is yours now, of course. And what do you mean to do with this shop of yours, now you have gained it?'

It would have to close, of course. But only a fool would begin that conversation right after the wedding. 'Now is not the appropriate time to speak of it,' he said.

'When, then?' she said, looking up into his face

with more interest and intensity than she had during the ceremony.

'I will tell you when I have come to a conclusion.' The conclusion was foregone. But it must be delivered in a way that would not lead to a screaming row in a public room.

'And until that time, what am I to tell my employees? There are seven people who...' She paused. 'Six people,' she amended. 'After whatever you said to him the other day, Mr Pratchet has fled.' She gave him a sharp look. 'It was most unhelpful of you. The lack of a skilled metal worker could severely limit the business I am able to do. I am training up a clever girl who had been working the back counter and sweeping the floor. But what is the point to designing, if there is no one there to execute—'

'You could not stand Fratchet,' he reminded her, purposely mispronouncing the name so she would not hear him stammer.

'That is not the point,' she said.

'You are b-better off without him.' The man had been in the thick of the true conspiracy against her. And today, she took his side against Stephen.

She looked at him in surprise. 'Jealousy does not suit you, Lord Fanworth.'

'I am not...' he began, and felt an annoying prickle of irritation at the thought of Pratchet's smug and possessive attitude towards Margot.

'You are,' she accused. 'It is why you are keeping me here, in the middle of a business day, when I should be working.'

'It is our wedding,' he pointed out, in what he thought was a reasonable way. 'When else would we have had it but the morning?'

'Any time we wished. You had a special licence. You were not limited to the conventional place and time. We could have married quietly, in the evening.'

'I sought to honour you,' he said, gritting his teeth.

'By taking me away from my work? We are short staffed in the front of the shop. And if I am gone as well?' She took a deep drink of her wine and set her napkin aside, pushing away from the table. 'The clerks have no idea how to go on without some kind of instruction. Yet, here I sit, with you, nibbling cake.'

Only a few weeks ago, she had been eager to take time out of her schedule to talk with him. Why was it so different now? Perhaps it was because, when he spoke to her now, his voice sounded very like the one the Duke of Larchmont might use to put a tradeswoman in her place. 'You have known this event was coming. You should have readied them for your absence.'

'Do you question my ability to run a business that has been in my family for generations?'

'I question the need for it,' he said, even more annoyed than he had been at the mention of Pratchet. 'You are my wife. You can do anything you wish. Yet you speak as if you mean to leave in the middle of your wedding feast to return to that shop.'

'I do,' she said. 'Two simple words, Lord Fanworth.'

For such a small answer, it cut like a knife. Even at his worst, she had never mocked him, before this moment. She had never smiled as he stuttered, or grown impatient as he struggled and tried to finish the sentence.

She had saved it for this moment, when it was

too late to get away. She had no right to speak so to the scion of one of the noblest families in Britain. 'You will return to my rooms as soon as the shop is closed.'

'To celebrate our wedding night?' She gave him another of her horribly blunt looks. 'At no time did I agree to that.'

'On the contrary. At the altar...'

'I believe the agreement already in place stated that I owe you two more nights, not a lifetime.'

'Things have changed.'

'Not as much as you seem to think,' she said. 'We married because my family left me no choice in the matter. But I like you even less than I did yesterday. If you insist, I will return to your rooms this evening. It will reduce the number of nights I must spend in your bed to one. I suggest you save it for a special occasion. A birthday, perhaps. Or Christmas.'

'Go!' His strength had returned to him in a rush of rage so strong it turned the command into a curse. But the relief was short lived. Suddenly, she chose to obey him, as a good wife should, and quit the room.

Chapter Thirteen

Margot stood behind a display in de Bryun's, tracing idle circles on the countertop with her finger. On the other side of the glass, gold wedding rings rested on satin, like so many shocked, round mouths and wide, round eyes. As if they had any right to judge her. What had just happened had definitely not been her dream of a perfect wedding day.

Of course, if she was truly honest, Margot could not remember ever dreaming of her wedding. She had not planned to get married at all. She had imagined herself, successful and alone. Not lonely, of course. Just, not married.

If someone had suggested that she might wed the son of a duke in Bath Abbey and follow it with a tasteful wedding breakfast in one of the most luxurious hotels in town, she'd have told them to stop spinning fairy tales.

Nor would she have expected to be devoid of wedding-night nerves, having dispensed with her virginity several weeks before the ceremony. In reality, this day was strangely anticlimactic.

The only real surprise was that it was possible to be even angrier with her new husband than she had been before. While he seemed fine with displaying her in a shop window at breakfast, there had been no sign of his family at either the wedding or the meal. He was ashamed of her.

To see her own ring placed on her finger, instead of some piece of family jewellery, was further proof that she was not worthy to be his marchioness. It was why, though she had sometimes dreamed of a proposal, she had not bothered to imagine a wedding. A union between them would not work.

Why did he still have that ring at all? Even after she had known him for the deceiver he'd proved to be, she'd assumed that he had bought her jewellery and requested her designs because he had some small respect for her talent. Even at the worst of times, it had done her good to think that the things he'd made adorned beautiful ladies of his acquaintance. Such a display would result in notoriety and more sales.

If he had kept the ring, what had happened to the rest of the things she had sold him?

'Will we be closing early today?' Jasper, the head clerk, looked hopefully at her.

'Why?' she said absently.

'Because of the wedding, your ladyship.'

She winced. 'Please, do not call me that.'

Now, the poor boy was utterly befuddled. 'I assumed, since it is proper… And you are not Miss de Bryun any more.'

Damn it all, he was right. She was no longer Miss de Bryun. But if she was not, then who was she and what name belonged on the shop window? She could not be Mrs Standish. When Fanworth had used his surname, it had seemed little better than a joke. But to become, without warning, a 'her ladyship' was too much to grasp on an already perplexing day.

She sighed. 'For now, perhaps it is better if you

do not call me anything at all. Simply state your business and I will do my best to answer you.'

'I asked about closing,' he reminded her.

There was really no reason to stay open, when the shop was as desperately empty as it had been lately. This afternoon, the only potential customers had done nothing more than to peer in the window, whisper to each other and hurry away. 'I suppose there is no reason to stay here doing nothing. You can all go home, at least. Since I was gone the better part of the morning, I should be the one to stay to close up.'

Jasper paused for a moment, then said, 'If I may be so bold, miss, uh, ma'am. There is no reason that you should have to make up lost time in your own shop. Why do you employ us, if not to make your labours lighter?' And then, to prove that matters were well in hand, he presented the ledger with the day's only transaction neatly recorded, so she might total it with the cash in the drawer.

He was right, she supposed. While she had informed Fanworth that the place was in chaos without her, it had seemed to run quite well. 'Very good,' Margot said, not sure how she felt about the success. 'And now,' she called out, to the room in general, 'you are all released for the day. I will see you tomorrow, of course.'

But for how long? At least, for a while, it was still hers. Once Fanworth asserted himself, there was no telling what would happen to it.

If she was lucky, he would forget all about it. Now that they no longer shared pleasant conversations in the back room and she had persuaded him to stop walking by the window, he might have no reason to visit the place. If she was smart, she would give him what he wanted in bed and try not to goad him as she had today at breakfast. If she did not call attention to them, he might not care about her activities during the day. For all she knew, he might be planning that they lead separate lives.

She could keep her business. And he could chat up women on the street, laughing and talking with them, just as he used to with her. She had no clue as to the identity of the stranger she had seen with him through the window of the dress shop. But it seemed, now that he'd trapped her, Fanworth was cultivating a new favourite. Her cheeks had burned with shame and jealousy, as she had come into the church today. Did that woman call him Mr Standish? Or was he simply 'Stephen' to her? Or perhaps an affectionate 'Fanworth' as she touched his arm and stared up at him?

Why couldn't he simply have been a rake? If he had seduced her, and left her, she'd have been broken-hearted. It would have been awful, of course. But it would have been tidy. She could have put her finger on a day in the calendar when he stopped visiting. And perhaps some time later there would be a day where she stopped caring about it.

But, no. He had been a gentleman about it. He had pretended to love her. Then he had pretended that her honour mattered enough to marry her. And then he had gone looking for another woman, leaving Margot as a loose end, an unfinished job, a knot that would never be tied.

The bell on the door jingled and startled her from the unpleasantness. But it was not a customer, it was Justine. It was just as well. Margot did not feel like smiling or being polite or helpful. She felt like stomping her foot and throwing things.

Was it obvious from her expression? Without another word, Justine stepped behind the counter and enveloped her in a sisterly embrace.

'Such a greeting,' she said, trying not to sound as vexed as she felt. 'We have only just seen each other, you know. The way you are hugging me, it might have been years.'

'It seems that way,' Justine admitted. 'For I have only just left the company of your husband. After you were gone, he did not say another word. Only drank his wine and stared at us.'

Margot laughed. 'However did you escape?'

'Eventually, Will threw his napkin to the floor and made a very rude apology. Then Fanworth stood and we left.' She reached out and offered another hug. 'I am so sorry.'

'Whatever for? You were the one who suffered his bad temper, I was the one who abandoned you to it.'

'I knew he was bad,' Justine admitted. 'But when Will spoke to him, he came away thinking that perhaps a marriage between you would work out well. I had no idea he would drink so, on his own wedding day.'

'A bottle of wine at the wedding breakfast is not so very much. And I did give him reason to be angry,' Margot said, surprised to be defending him.

'If only the wine were all,' her sister said, with a disappointed sigh. 'I had no idea that he would arrive at the church so foxed he could not manage the vows.'

At this, Margot laughed. 'You thought he was drunk?'

'How else to explain the fact that he could not say the few simple words he had promised to?'

'He could not speak because he stammers,' she said, amazed that her sister did not know it already. 'Bs and Ds are especially bad. When he learned our last name...' The poor man had been tongue-tied. 'I gave him permission to call me Margot,' she said, remembering his smile of relief.

Then he had offered to make her Mrs Standish, for convenience's sake, if nothing else. They had laughed together over it. When he had left, she had blushed for the rest of the afternoon.

'That cannot be,' Justine said. 'We have all seen him, here, and in London, and no one has mentioned it before.'

'That is because he does not talk if he does not have to,' Margot said, stating the obvious. 'Have you never noticed how carefully he chooses his words? He avoids that which he cannot say. But when he has no choice, as in the church today...'

It must have been horrible for him. Then, over breakfast, she had taunted him with it. Suddenly, the anger inside her turned to shame. Whatever he had done to her, she had no right to attack him over something that pained him as deeply as this did, especially since he had no control over it.

Justine was still doubtful. 'How do you know of this, if none of us have seen it? Will's brother, Bellston, has known the man for years and has nothing to say about him other than to announce that he—' She broke off, embarrassed.

Margot gave her an expectant look.

'That he was almost as big a prig as his father, Larchmont,' Justine finished.

At this, Margot laughed. 'None of you know him as well as I do.' She stopped, surprised. She had said that without thinking. But if she was the only person who had noticed his stutter, it was probably true. Until the problem with the necklace, she'd have sworn that the real Stephen Standish was a complicated man, by turns roguish, funny, gallant and passionate.

And then, suddenly, everything had changed. Why had he turned so cold to her, treating her like a stranger? It would have made sense, if he actually believed any of the things he had accused her of...

Justine was staring at her, probably confused by her silence. 'Well, if you seriously think you know him, then perhaps there is hope. But my offer still stands. If you think you have reason to avoid his home or his bed, then come to me. You will be welcome.'

'Thank you,' Margot said. 'But I think, for now at least, things will be fine as they are.' No matter how bad it might be, she would not be running to her sister with her problems. If there was anything to be done that would make a marriage easier between her and her new husband, it would have to be decided between the two of them.

When Justine left, it was time to close up for the evening. Margot looked with longing at the little flight of stairs that led to her apartments above the shop. How easy it would be to forget about the morning and simply climb them, to put her tea on in the little kitchen and go to sleep in her narrow but comfortable bed?

Only to have Fanworth come and haul her out of it, she supposed. Even if she had not promised to return to him, her discussion with Justine left her feeling unsettled. When he had been sweet and kind to her, she thought she'd understood him. Then he had been cruel. But she was still sure she understood his reason for it.

Now she was lost again. The laughing, kind Stephen Standish had been real. Given his unwillingness to reveal his impediment to the world, he'd never have paraded it before her, simply to get her to bed. But then, why had he changed? Had Mr Pratchet lied about his involvement? But then, where had the rubies come from?

Thinking about it made her head hurt. Or perhaps it was the lack of a decent meal. If she had swallowed her pride along with her share of the wedding breakfast, at least she might not be hungry.

If there was no supper waiting for her, she would insist that something be brought to her room. If she went to her husband's bed tonight, there was no reason to let nerves prevent her from eating. The worst was over. Her maidenhead was gone and what they were about to do was sanctioned by church and society.

And, if she was perfectly honest with herself, it might be enjoyable. Her whole body trembled when she thought of the last time she had lain with him. Despite what she had said to him at breakfast, she looked forward to doing it again, without guilt. It would be even better if there was a chance that she might find her way back to the Stephen she had fallen in love with.

Then she remembered the girl in the street. She might pine for their former familiarity. But it seemed he had moved on to another.

As she shut the front door of the shop and locked it, a black carriage pull forward, from the corner. 'Your ladyship?'

She glanced at the crest on the door and the colours of livery. She had not seen it before, but it must be Fanworth's. Her new family colours. She turned to the groom.

The man bowed. 'Lord Fanworth sent us to retrieve you. If you are ready, of course.'

She could argue that she preferred to walk, but what would be the point, other than to make life more difficult for this poor man? 'Thank you.' She allowed him to help her into a seat for the short ride to Fanworth's apartment.

And today, when she entered, it was through the front door. The look on Mrs Sims's face was still not what Margot would call welcoming. But at least the woman held her tongue as she took Margot's bonnet and cloak, and escorted her up the stairs.

Things had changed since her last visit. When the door opened, she had expected to see Fanworth's private sitting room. Instead, most of the furniture had been removed and his bed and dresser had been moved into the space they'd occupied.

Margot raised an eyebrow.

'Your room is through here, your ladyship.' The

housekeeper led the way through the changing room, to what had been the master bedroom, then turned and abandoned her to her fate.

When that woman had said it was *her room*, it had not been a generalisation. All traces of masculinity had been scrubbed from it. The walls and the windows were hung with cream silk and the large bed had a matching satin coverlet and chiffon curtains that would be useless to keep out the morning light. Since she was often up before the sun, it probably didn't matter.

It appeared that the decorations had been chosen to remind her of the shop. If so, it was a confusing message. Was it to remind her that her new job lay here, in this bed? Or was it simply an effort to design a room to suit her tastes?

She opened the nearest cupboard and found the dresses she had ordered while shopping with Justine. Apparently, the woman had saved time and sent them directly to her new home. Which meant the drawers on the dresser must contain the scandalous nightclothes that Justine had made for her wedding night.

When she had thought of this moment, over

the last few weeks, she had envisaged her things stacked haphazardly in the corner of the room, a reminder that their owner did not quite fit in this new world that had been forced upon her.

She had been quite wrong. For someone she suspected of marrying her as little more than an afterthought, Fanworth had taken surprising care to make her feel welcome in her new life.

'Is it suitable?' He stood behind her, in the doorway to his own room, and had been watching her reaction. 'The entry to the hall is not yet finished. The carpenters were late.' He pointed to a place on the wall.

He meant a doorway, she supposed. But he had been careful not to say the word in front of her, for fear of a stutter. It made her strangely sad. 'It is lovely,' she said.

'They are setting a meal on the table in my room. If you wish...' He did not finish.

'Of course. Thank you.'

Once the food was served, the housekeeper disappeared, leaving them alone together for the first time in their married life. If she had expected Fanworth to relax, she was mistaken. If possible, he became even more quiet, as he ate from the plate set in front of him without so much as a clink of cutlery.

She tasted her own food, then set down her fork, reached for her wine and took a hurried sip. It appeared that Fanworth's cook was of the sort that was heavy handed with seasonings. The capon on her plate was so salty as to be practically inedible. She tried the carrots beside it only to discover where the pepper had been used. To make up for the two of them, the potatoes had not been seasoned at all, only burnt dry. She glanced at her husband who was close to clearing his plate without comment. 'How was your food?'

'Excellent, as usual,' he said, but made no effort to elaborate.

Either the man had no taste at all or she had been sent another subtle message of disapproval from the household staff. To test her theory, she reached for the dessert course, which was a shared pot du crème, garnished with berries. It was exquisite. She gathered it to herself and stuck in her spoon without bothering to fill her plate.

He watched her for a moment as if trying to

decide if the behaviour had significance or was an aberration in manners worthy of correction. Then he reached for her plate, tasted her food and immediately spat into his napkin. This was followed by a torrent of perfectly pronounced cursing and the same foul look he must have given to her family over breakfast.

Then he rose and turned to the bell pull.

'No.' She put her hand on his arm to draw him back down.

'This cannot stand,' he said, waving his hand at her plate.

'It can wait until tomorrow.' She had almost said, *do not ruin tonight*. But she had no proof that statement was appropriate. It was quite possible that there was nothing left of the day to be salvaged.

He sat down again, still irritated. But since his mood was in defence of her, she did not mind it so very much. Then he switched their plates, offering her what little was left on his and setting a buttered roll beside it.

'Thank you,' she said, too hungry to pretend that his sacrifice had not been necessary. She tasted and found he was right. The food was excellent, if the cook liked and respected the one being served. That was some consolation. It would be far easier to deal with a tantrum in the kitchen than complete incompetence.

Fanworth's act of kindness was a silent one. He made no effort to comment further on the staff, the day, or his plans for the night. He simply stuck his spoon into the opposite side of the custard and ate.

It was clear he had no intention of volunteering information. If she wanted answers, she must find the questions that would most easily coax the truth out of him. He set down the custard bowl and took a sip of wine, watching her over the rim of the glass. She did not need words to guess what he was thinking about. His gaze had a confidence that had been absent in church.

She felt a low burn in her belly at the way his eyes travelled over her skin. And, for a moment, she actually wished she was wearing one of the new dinner gowns that would bare her shoulders so he might stare at them. Perhaps then he would feel as distracted as she felt. If she was not careful, by the time the meal ended, they would be in bed and she would have learned nothing.

She wet her lips. 'May I ask you something?'

'I cannot stop you,' he said, with the faintest of smiles.

She grasped one hand in the other, twisting her wedding ring off her finger and handing it back to him. 'Why did you give me this?'

'It was made for you.'

It had not been. She should know for she had taken the specifications herself. Though, if she was honest, she had been loath to let this piece go. He had encouraged her to create a ring no woman could resist and she had used her own tastes as a guide. But to wear it herself defeated the purpose. 'Surely there was some family ring that was meant for the woman you were to marry.'

She had almost said, 'For me.' But none of the Larchmont entail was intended for the likes of her. They both knew it.

He set the ring on the table next to his glass and went to his dresser. He returned with a wooden jewellery box, dumping the contents on the cloth beside her plate. Then he rooted through the pile with the tip of his finger before producing a ring. 'This.'

She picked it up and examined it with the critical eye of a jeweller. The setting was too large for the stone, which was an inferior grade of opal so old it was losing its fire. Opals were bad luck in wedding rings, for exactly that reason. If the lustre signified the spirit of the wearer, this spoke of a fading soul.

'Ugly, isn't it?' he said.

'It is,' she agreed, unable to lie.

He reached forward and gathered her hand in his, then picked up the ring and slipped it back on to her finger. 'This is not.'

So it had not been an insult at all. 'When you bought pieces from me, what did you do with them?'

He went back to his dresser and retrieved another box, this one a lustrous ebony. When he opened it, the pieces she had sold him were nestled in the white-silk lining.

'You did not give them away,' she said, numb with disappointment.

'Who would I have given them to?' he replied

with a half-smile rather like the one she remembered from the shop.

'You spoke of an actress, a mistress, cousins…'

'I needed a reason to frequent the shop,' he said, as though pleased with his own cleverness. 'I saved them. For you.'

No one had seen them. No one at all. She had worked so hard to make them perfect, knowing that the woman on the arm of a marquess would draw all eyes in a room. They would see her jewels and whisper. Then they would come to de Bryun's.

And all this time, they had been hidden in his bedroom, invisible. Now he was staring at her, as though waiting for her to be grateful for the gift.

'They were meant to be worn, not locked away in a box,' she said softly. 'I'd hoped that people would admire them and ask about the jeweller. It would bring more business.'

'People will see them now,' he said. 'On the Marchioness of Fanworth.'

Then she might as well put them back in the box and take them to the shop for resale. She had no time to parade about Bath in the evenings like a walking advertisement.

'You never wear j-jewels,' he added. 'You should.'

'I am surrounded by them all day,' she said, with a sigh.

'Exactly,' he said, as if they were in some way finding a common ground. 'Yet you act as if you are not worthy of them.'

How could she explain that it had never been her desire to wear the things she made? Granted, the ring was attractive. She had designed it to be so. But she had never imagined it on her own hand.

He took her silence for assent and reached into the tumbled pile of jewels, slowly drawing forth a string of pearls and draping it around her neck. It was a long rope with a gold and diamond clasp in the shape of joined hands. It was beautiful, of course, but it did not suit her. Even when wrapped three or more times about her neck it would still be too long for the modest gown she was wearing.

'Where is the lace?' he said with a slight frown, tracing the neckline with a finger.

He meant Justine's fichu, she supposed. 'I left it at the shop. It was in the way.'

'It was lovely.' He shrugged. 'Not as lovely as you, of course.' Then he took her by the hand and pulled her to her feet, to stand before a full-length mirror beside his bed.

And so it was to begin. She had convinced herself that she was not nervous. It had been a lie. A few compliments and a touch of his hand, and her pulse was racing. Knowing what was to come had removed the fear from her wedding night. But dread had been replaced with eager anticipation.

He stood behind her now, loosening the back of her gown, until her shoulders and throat were bare and the pearls could rest against them.

'Luminous, like moonlight,' he said, tracing them with his finger. 'But they are no match for your skin.' He placed his palm flat on the beads, rolling them against her bare throat.

Despite her unwillingness to wear them, she enjoyed the feel of the pearls pressing into her flesh and the roll against her tired shoulders. He released the loop he had been holding and let it slither under the bodice until it swayed between her breasts. Then his hands were behind her again, undoing more hooks and laces until she stood bare before the mirror with her bodice, stays and shift bunched at her waist.

He took up the pearls again, rolling them up the slope of one of her breasts, sliding them back and forth across her nipple. 'Now tell me, how do you like your own work?'

They were not really her work at all. Though she had made the clasp, the oyster had supplied the majority of this perfection. She had but given them order. But words failed her. Her reflection showed a ring of pearls about her breast. As he tugged on it and as the loop tightened, the skin around her nipple tightened as well. His hand cupped the other breast from beneath, the tip of it pinched firmly between ring and last finger.

He pressed kisses into her shoulder, until his lips rested warm against her ear. 'I want to take you wearing nothing but pearls.'

He had not stuttered. How strange. But everything about this was strange. She was staring at her own body in a mirror, watching him touch it, hardly daring to breathe for fear he would stop.

Now she was helping him as he pushed the skirts to the floor. He settled her own hand to the wet place between her legs so that she could touch herself as she watched the pearls sway against her belly.

It was wicked. It was decadent. And she loved it. She rubbed her back against the wool of his coat for it seemed to heighten the sensation of her own hand to know he was there, hungry eyed, watching her pleasure herself. Her breath caught in her throat as the first tremors of arousal began.

Suddenly, he released her to fumble with the buttons of his breeches. Then he thrust into her hard, over and over. His hands came back to her breasts to hold her so tight to his body that her feet barely touched the floor.

Her self-control snapped, and she reached behind her to clutch at the back of his thighs. Her body tightened to grip his shaft, as if she could draw him into her very soul and keep him there for ever.

It was over too soon. His fingers relaxed their grip on her and his head lolled forward so that his hair brushed against her arm. Then he gave a final sigh of satisfaction and scooped her up in his arms to carry her into the other room and drop her on the satin coverlet.

Without a second thought, she held out an arm to welcome him into her bed.

He shook his head. 'Only one time left. I must be careful.' But he did not leave. And then he smiled.

She had been angry with him this morning. In turn, he had been furious with her. It was possible, once they regained their senses, that they would be right back to sniping at each other.

But that did not alter the fact that she wanted more.

She ran a finger along the rope of pearls, tracing them from her neck to the low point where they settled on her belly. Then, she spread her legs.

He stared at her for a moment, doubtful. 'I suppose I could stay. For a while.'

She nodded. Then she smiled as he began to remove his clothing. He looked rather undignified, standing over her with his breeches hanging open. But it would not last. The Marquess of Fanworth was never without his dignity. She would cherish the brief loss of control, for she might not see it again.

Now he was fully nude. The sight of him made her forget that she longed for vulnerability. Like this, he was invincible. The long smooth flanks, narrow waist and strange ridges of muscle made her long to touch and to submit. If she could capture such fluid power in gold, she would worship at it, like a pagan.

She smiled to herself at the ridiculousness of the idea. But the sight of him stirred something in her, other than simple lust. It was the strange, creative rush she got, right before a new idea. Tomorrow, when she got to the shop, she would take up her sketch pad and see what resulted.

But for tonight?

He was climbing up on to the bed with her, lying on his side, his head leaning against his bent arm. Then, he leaned forward and kissed her. It was more tender than passionate and his smile was achingly familiar. It belonged to Stephen Standish: the man she loved.

His free hand reached to brush the hair from

her face. 'Lady Fanworth,' he said softly, 'you are temptation incarnate.'

If that was so, then for a change he was at her mercy and she could do as she wished with him. So she slipped the pearls from about her neck, wrapped them loosely around his manhood and stroked.

Chapter Fourteen

Stephen awoke the next morning to the smell of lavender and the feel of satin against his cheek. It took him a moment to realise that he was face-down in the pillows of his wife's bed. He had requested the linen be pressed with flowers and chosen the coverlet himself. It was to be the sort of gentle bower his beloved deserved.

Despite his careful planning, she had left him again, to go to that damnable shop. It had never occurred to him that, when offered wealth, title and a life of ease, the woman he married might continue to work. It was a nice enough shop, he supposed. He had found his visits to the white-velvet salon to be relaxing and pleasant.

But then the place had not been his rival. When he thought of it, he felt something very like jealousy. It was clear that she loved it more than she did him. And she gave no indication of changing her mind on that point.

The current situation could not continue. He had no real wish to command her to give up her work and stay in his home. If she chose to do so of her own accord, life would be better for both of them. But to achieve that, he must give her a reason to stay.

His intent had been to wake before she did and be ready to stop her as she passed by his bed on her way to the door. If she could be tempted with the pleasures of the marital bed, she might forget all about the desire to rush away from him, just to stand behind a glass-topped counter, smiling at strangers.

He had intended to do that. Instead, he had overslept. To be fair, she had exhausted him. One of her silk stockings was tied about his wrist in remembrance of a point during the previous evening when he had tried to leave her. His other hand clutched those infernal pearls.

He set them gently on the pillow, as if they were a dangerous weapon that could discharge at any moment. He had thought to tease her with them. But she had turned the tables upon him, binding him with them until excitement made the tightness a mix of pleasure and pain. Then she'd released him and he'd surged into her, desperate for relief.

At least she seemed to have forgotten her threat to hold him to their earlier agreement. If she meant to set a strict limit of four encounters, they would need to reason like Jesuits to explain last night. At the very least, he would insist that some of the things they had done to celebrate their wedding could count for a half, or perhaps a quarter of a whole.

Of course, some had been so delightful they should be counted twice. If some creativity was not used in the accounting, the rest of his marriage would be had on credit.

He hoped that her ardour was a sign that her resolve was weakening. If she would warm to him enough to listen, he was more than willing to apologise for the trouble he had caused her. She would be more likely to believe him if he could have got Pratchet to retract his slander. But there was no hope of that. Stephen had taken too much pleasure in frightening him and, as expected, the little man had bolted.

The alternative was to force Arthur to explain himself. But if his brother wanted revenge for his damaged nose, it would be most unwise to introduce him to Margot.

He'd find another way, then. But damned if he knew what.

It had been an interesting night.

Margot stood behind the counter, staring off into space, unwilling to wipe the small, secret smile from her face. It was clear that marriage had advantages. She had filled several pages of her sketchbook with ideas for new designs, including a fob chain with links that reminded her of the crook in her husband's elbow.

Then she set Miss Ross up with the form and the heaviest gauge of gold wire, teaching her how to twist as she wrapped it to add character to a plain chain. It was a simple enough construction and it would be a useful skill for the girl to form and cut links and solder them back together.

Perhaps some new designs in the front window would help to draw trade. She had been an object of curiosity when she was Fanworth's mistress. People came to the shop so they might gossip about her. Many of them made purchases so their motives might be less obvious.

But the moment that it was announced she was to be his wife, the crowds had dispersed. The world could not decide what to do with a marchioness who was in trade. Were they to scrape and bow to her, or should she do it to them? So far, society had decided she was neither fish nor fowl, therefore, it was best to push her to the side of the plate and ignore her.

But just now, there was a fashionable lady, passing by on the other side of the street. Perhaps she was in need of a gift for a lover or a husband? Then the woman passed from shade into sunlight and adjusted the angle of her parasol so Margot could see her face.

Not her.

She needed customers. But of all the women in Bath, this one must just keep walking. It was the beautiful woman who had been speaking with

Fanworth, the week before their marriage. More importantly, she was the one to whom Stephen had had been speaking.

Even during last night's intimacy, when speaking to her he'd seemed to navigate with caution. He had spoken little, but when he'd smiled, he'd seemed almost like his old self. It had been going so well that she hoped, just maybe, he might relax and be the man she once loved.

But at the sight of this woman, Margot's confidence slipped. He might have married her, but that did not mean that he intended to open his heart to her. If there was to be a relationship between this woman and Stephen, it was not her place to comment on it. Perhaps, if he was distracted, he would be less likely to interfere in the shop. Perhaps he would forget about her, and it, and things could go back to the way they had been.

Suddenly, that prospect did not seem nearly as inviting as it would have, before last night.

And now the last woman in the world whom Margot wished to see had crossed the street and was passing by the shop again, pausing at the front window to stare directly in at her.

Margot offered a polite smile in response. It would not do to scowl at a potential customer. Nor would it help either of them if she admitted recognition of the woman who was likely to steal her husband's attention, just as she realised she still wanted it.

The young lady came very near to passing by again before turning back, as though she wished the nerve to enter, but hadn't quite mustered it. She was young enough to be unsure of herself. Now that Margot could see her clearly, it was plain that this girl was no older than herself. Young and lovely, with smooth brown hair, large clear eyes and the limbs of a colt.

The maid following patiently behind her spoke of a family rich enough to make sure there was money in her pocket for frivolity.

Margot forced another, even brighter smile through the glass, holding her breath. *Go*, Margot willed silently. *Or come, if you must. But do not linger in the street, staring at me. You will embarrass us both.*

The girl smiled as well. She hesitated for a moment longer, then made her decision and reached for the shop door, giving it a sharp pull. The brass bell clanked and she looked up in alarm, as though fearing she'd caused an affront.

'Welcome,' Margot said softly. 'May I be of assistance?'

'Are you Lady Fanworth?' the girl asked hopefully.

Margot took care to hide the chagrin at hearing the unfamiliar title. Then she offered a brief nod.

'I attempted to call on you at home, but they told me that you would be here.' She pulled a card case from her reticule and searched around her for some servant who she might hand it to. Then she put it away again, still torn between etiquette and the simpler rules that should preside here. 'I am Louisa,' she said. When the name had no effect, she added, 'Standish. Fanworth's sister.'

Of course. It was why they had been so well suited, when they had stood on the street together. And why he had talked easily and laughed with her.

But it did not explain why he'd said nothing of the meeting. And why had she not come to the wedding if she had been here in Bath, all along? The hurt came back, fresh and sharp.

She swallowed it and put on her most neutral smile. Louisa Standish was here, now. The least Margot could do was pretend that it was a normal meeting. 'Come in Lady Louisa. Please. Sit down with me. Perhaps a glass of lemonade, or perhaps a ratafia, in the back salon.'

Lady Louisa gave her a hopeful smile. 'You have the time?'

'For you? For family?' Margot added, the words thick on her tongue. 'Of course.' She held back the drapery and escorted the girl to the same *chaise* that her brother had so often enjoyed, and snapped her fingers to an idle clerk, indicating that refreshments must be brought.

Then she stared at Lady Louisa for a moment, trying to clear the haze from her brain. What was she to make of this visit? It was too late for the girl to upbraid her for angling after a man so far above her station. But there was nothing in her manner that suggested that was the reason for the visit. Still, it was strange that their first meeting was here and not in the Abbey.

Louisa looked at her with an equally dazed expression. 'We are all very curious about the new member of the family, but rather at a loss as to how to proceed,' she said, with the shyest of smiles. 'Well, Mother is. She very much wants to meet you. But without my brother's permission, she cannot. And, of course, he will not give that.' She gave a little shake of her head, to indicate that there was nothing to be done with some people. 'In my opinion, Fanworth can hardly be blamed for any of it. But, since they have all but forgotten about me, I decided to take matters into my own hands.' She extended her hands outward in a gesture that said, 'Here we are'.

'Blamed for any of what?' Margot gave up trying to pretend that any of it made sense to her.

'Why, not inviting the family to your wedding,' she said, as though it must be totally apparent.

Margot sniffed. 'I understand that your family is probably mortified. But if he was so embarrassed by me, he really needn't have bothered with the wedding.'

Louisa's eyes grew wide. 'Is that what you thought? Oh, dear.' She shook her head. 'And he allowed you to labour under this misapprehension.' She shook her head again. 'Stephen is my favourite brother, Lady Fanworth. In fact, he is my favourite person in the entire world. But you must have noticed how stubborn he is and how proud.'

'It is why he does not speak,' Margot agreed.

'I had hoped he would, at least, speak to the woman he chose to marry.'

He had. Once. What could she tell her husband's sister that did not make it sound as if she did not know the man at all? For she was beginning to think, perhaps she didn't. 'It was all very rushed,' she said, striking a path between explanation and apology. 'And certainly not the wedding that either of us expected to have.' She glanced around the shop, angry that they might expect her to be ashamed of all that she had accomplished. 'But I am sure I am not the woman that Lord Fanworth expected to present to his family.'

'On the contrary,' Louisa insisted. 'He spoke most highly of you and was eager for us to meet, even though he did not wish me to attend the wedding. He extolled your beauty, your wit and your talent. He said we would get on famously, once he had found a way to introduce us.' She smiled. 'It was a great relief to know that his heart was engaged. I have never seen him so effusive.'

'He was effusive?' It explained the animated conversation she had witnessed in the street. But it had never occurred to her that she might have been the topic discussed. It was even more surprising that he had been numbering her many good qualities. Given that, it made no sense that he should prohibit his sister from attending, if he was so very fond of the pair of them. 'I am afraid I still do not understand. If I am such a catch, then why did you not at least take breakfast with us yesterday?'

Lady Louisa gave her a sad smile. 'It is simple. He is not ashamed of you, Lady Fanworth. He is ashamed of us.'

'Of you?'

'Well not me, perhaps,' Louisa admitted. 'We really do get along brilliantly. But I could not come without Mother. Mother would have insisted that Father be invited, before she was willing to attend. She still hopes there is a way to mend this breach between the duke and his heir.' Louisa shook her head as though contemplating the impossible.

'My husband does not get on with his father? If anything, society seems to think they are two of a kind.'

'Heavens, no. They are both proud, of course. But that is because of Father's continual reminders that the Larchmont title is one of the oldest and most respectable in Britain. Nothing must be done to embarrass the family.' Louisa frowned. 'Although he claims to want the best for his heir, he actually wants the best *from* him as well. Nothing less than perfection will do.'

'And Stephen is not perfect,' Margot said, hating even to mention a thing which did not really matter.

'When Father is disappointed...' Louisa gave her a tight, little smile '...it is best to just avoid him. Since he is frequently disappointed in Stephen, my brother refuses to have anything to do with him.' She whispered the next, as though it were part of some shameful secret. 'The stammering is really so much better than he used to be, now that they do not talk. When Stephen was at home, if he made even the smallest mistake, Father would badger him until he could not talk at all.'

It was a horrible story. But it explained why the church had stood empty on their wedding day. 'So there could be no duchess without a duke, and no you without the duchess.' She thought for a moment. 'But I understand you have a second brother, as well?'

Louisa nodded. 'At the moment, there is a disagreement of some kind between my brothers. Fanworth was adamant that he did not want to see Arthur at his wedding. And Arthur does not want to be seen by anyone until the bruises have fully healed.'

'Bruises,' Margot repeated, still confused.

'Stephen struck him,' Louisa said with a little giggle. 'I think his nose is broken. And both eyes...' She gulped back a full laugh and took a ladylike sip of her drink to clear her throat. 'I do not know exactly why. But I am sure that there was a good reason for it. Fanworth likes to pretend that he is gruff and imposing. But he is not usually moved to violence. And Arthur?' Louisa sighed. 'Arthur frequently deserves to be hit. At one time or another, we are all disappointed in him. Yet, Father seems to like him best of all. There is no pleasing some people and that is that.'

'You seem to have a most unusual family,' Margot said, as politely as possible.

'Perhaps that is true. Some say the upper classes are prone to eccentricity. If so, there are few houses that can compete with Larchmont.'

'If your father is so set on perfection, I suspect it makes your brother's choice of wife all the more unacceptable,' Margot said, resigned to her role.

'Perhaps you did not understand my meaning,' Louisa said with another little sigh. 'There is no woman likely to find acceptance in a family led by my father. The fact that she was chosen by Stephen would be reason enough for him to find fault.' Then she smiled. 'For my part, I love my brother very much. If he loves you, that is reason enough for me to love you, as well.'

Now Margot should explain that it was not a love match at all. Despite what Louisa had told her of their conversation, she suspected her husband barely tolerated her when she was not in his bed. But when she was? Her skin grew hot at the thought of the previous night's sport.

Perhaps that was a solid basis for a marriage and the rest did not matter. And to see this lovely young woman smiling before her and holding out the family olive branch was too tempting. 'If you welcome me, of course we will be friends,' Margot said cautiously.

'Or sisters, if you wish,' Louisa said, with a hopeful smile.

'I already have a sister,' Margot responded, then noticed the other woman's smile falter. 'But that is no reason that I cannot have another one.'

Louisa smiled again. 'I have never had one. And few friends because…Father,' she said as if that explained it all. 'Mother is a dear, of course. But there are times it would be nice to have someone nearer my own age.' She glanced around her. 'Even if you are so often here.'

'I work here,' Margot said, testing her reaction to the word. 'But since I am the owner, I could be a bit more free with my time.' Hadn't Jasper suggested such a thing just yesterday? Perhaps the world would not end if she was not here from dawn to dusk. 'When your brother used to visit here, I spent many happy hours talking with him.'

'Talking. With. Fanworth.' Louisa's first expression was one of incredulity. Then it settled into a warm smile. 'Of course. I think this makes everything much clearer. When Mother heard how beautiful you were, she was rather worried.' She stood, ready to take her leave. 'But I will tell Mother that you have talked with Fanworth, for hours at a time. It will set her mind at rest.'

Margot stood as well and returned a smile to this rather cryptic remark, not wanting to think too hard on what the duchess had assumed about her character. 'Thank you for your visit. And your kind words.'

'And thank you, for the sake of my brother.' Louisa smiled again. 'I will come again, soon. If that is all right.'

'Of course.' Margot escorted her to the door. As she waved goodbye and watched Louisa and her maid stroll down the street, she felt more hopeful about her future than before, but no less confused.

Chapter Fifteen

Stephen spread the afternoon mail out on the writing desk in the salon and sighed. The packet of letters was not as large as he would have hoped. After his recent marriage, there should be invitations to balls, routs, or at least a dinner or two. Most importantly, there should be something addressed to Lady Fanworth.

Hopefully, Margot would not notice the degree to which she'd been snubbed. So far, the only event they would be attending was the hastily arranged reception Justine was hosting to celebrate the wedding and to welcome her brother-in-law, the Duke of Bellston, to Bath.

His parents would be in town by then. If they attended, it would give him a chance to introduce the family on neutral ground. Mother would

be charming wherever they met her. But Larchmont was more likely to be civil if another peer
was present. Much to his father's annoyance, the
Bellston title was the older and respect for tradi-
tion would force him to be on his best behaviour.

If the rest of the town did not see this party as
a reason to welcome them, then they could all be
damned. Since the majority of the *ton* followed
the Regent to Brighton, it hardly mattered what
people thought here. They would manage well
enough until it was time to retire to Derbyshire
and by the London Season, it would be old news.

But while he could ignore the snubs of strangers, he would not abide dissension in the staff.
When he had come on holiday, he'd brought Mrs
Simms, and the cook along with him. He liked his
comforts and, in Derbyshire, those two women
fussed over him like two hens with a single chick.

But it appeared that his marrying a woman of
a lower class did not meet with their approval.
Worse yet, he had entertained her in his home
before marriage and they knew for a fact that she
was not as virginal as her snowy-white gowns.

The insults to his wife were subtle, but frequent. Mrs Sims had been able to keep her own counsel while he'd entertained Margot as a mistress in the house she managed. But her patience had come to an end the moment he announced he would be marrying her. At any mention of the wedding or the bride, Mrs Simms had taken to sniffing in disapproval. She had done it so often that he had enquired of her whether she had a cold, or some chronic condition that affected her breathing.

Cook was little better. Lady Fanworth's portion of last night's wedding supper had been practically inedible, as if she thought that it might be possible to starve the interloper out of the house. It was only Margot's kind-heartedness that had saved the pair of them from a dressing down worthy of Larchmont at his most temperamental.

As it sometimes was with servants, the lady's compassion was greeted with more contempt than obedience. And now they were growing so careless as to be gossiping in the front hall, oblivious to the fact that the master of the house was listening to every word.

'I suppose it will be dinner in the bedroom,

again,' said Cook in a disgusted voice, 'while a perfectly good dining room stands empty.'

'Herself is too busy to use it,' Mrs Sims responded, equally annoyed. 'Down to that shop, dawn until dusk.'

'Perhaps I should ask her to stop at the grocer's on her way home,' Cook said with an evil chuckle.

'It makes more sense than that we be waiting on her,' Mrs Sims agreed. 'A tradesman's daughter. No better than us, really. The duke will never approve. Of course, her Grace's blood is as blue as the Princess Charlotte's.'

Stephen rose, throwing down the letter he had been holding. By God, he had heard more than enough. They had served in the family since before his birth. But he would sack the pair of them if this was how they behaved when he was not in the room.

'Ladies.' Margot had heard as well. She had come home hours earlier than usual, totally unprepared for a household contretemps. If he'd handled the problem last night, as he should have, he might have saved her from this embarrassing encounter.

'Your ladyship,' both women responded in unison and there was a moment of silence to cover what must have been the most hypocritical curtsies ever performed.

Stephen waited for his wife's response. Had his mother ever been in such a situation? He doubted it. She held the staff in check as Lord Nelson held the Navy. But then, she was past fifty and had been the daughter of an earl before becoming a duchess. If his sister had been presented with such a problem, it would have reduced her to tears.

And Margot was barely older than Louise.

'Despite the concerns you voiced a moment ago, dinner will be in the dining room tonight,' Margo said. 'And so it will be on any evening I arrive before six. I trust that it will not be necessary for me to run errands, since Fanworth assures me that his house is very well managed.'

Liar. They had never discussed such a thing. He smiled.

She sighed so heavily that he could hear it from where he sat. 'But I begin to wonder if that is the case. Last night, the capon you left for me was practically inedible. It was as if someone had upended the salt cellar over it. There was too much pepper in the carrots and the potatoes were bland. Fanworth shared his plate with me and neither of us got enough to eat. See that it does not happen again.'

'Yes, your ladyship,' said Cook, properly chastised.

'And before we go any further, Mrs Sims, I must correct your other assessment of me. I am not a tradesman's daughter.'

'You are not?' Now the woman was torn between bravado and confusion.

'I am something far worse.' It was said in a sweet and youthful voice that hardly matched her matter-of-fact tone. 'My father has been dead for over twenty years. I own and run the business alone. I am in trade myself, Mrs Sims. As such I am accustomed to dealing with employees, both hiring and firing.' She took another dramatic pause. Then she continued. 'Perhaps other young ladies of my age would be intimidated by your obvious mastery of the household. But I am not. I respect it, of course. And Fanworth adores you. It would be a shame to have to replace either of you. But I will do so without hesitation if you are unwilling or unable to take my instructions.'

'Of course, your ladyship.' There was a kind of grudging respect in Mrs Sims's answer, as though she had not expected the new lady of the house to have such starch in her.

'Very good.' Through it all, Margot's voice had lost none of its cheerfulness. 'Dinner at seven, then. Send up a maid, for I intend to dress. And remember, do not over-salt the meat.'

'Yes, your ladyship.' This answer came in unison, as both women acknowledged her authority.

Then Margot was gone. The sound of her slippers pattering up the stairs was light, youthful and unladylike.

Stephen smiled and settled back into his chair.

As requested, dinner was served promptly at seven. Lady Fanworth looked well satisfied with herself and sent her compliments to the cook on an excellent meal. Then she smiled at him more warmly than she had in weeks.

Stephen smiled at her in return. For all he cared, they might have been eating gruel. He'd still have proclaimed it ambrosia. To see her smiling across the table at him was the fulfilment of the dream he'd harboured since the first day they met. And no part of that fantasy had prepared him for the sight of her, dressed for dinner.

Perhaps Bath society thought they could spurn her, as a lower-class woman who'd got above herself. But they had not seen her like this. She was perfection: her beauty unrivalled, her grace unaffected and her smile so warm and genuine that one could not help but be drawn to her. One had but to speak to her for a few moments to learn that her personality matched her looks. God made a woman once or twice in a generation who was fit to be a queen. It was only natural that Stephen should wish to make her a duchess.

And on a much more personal note, it was dizzyingly erotic to see her perfect shoulders displayed above the low neckline of her green-silk gown. He had kissed those shoulders. She wore the pearls around her throat to remind him that they had done far more than kiss. They would do so again tonight. He was, truly, the luckiest man in England.

She was staring at him as if she knew a secret. Her sea-green eyes were bottomless. He could gaze into them for the rest of his life, floating, sinking, lost in their depths.

She had spoken.

He had not heard. He dragged himself back to reality. 'Excuse me?'

'I said, I had a most interesting day at the shop today.'

'Really.'

'Your sister came to visit me.'

He could not even manage am abbreviated answer. All words were shocked out of him and he could do nothing but stare at her in silence.

'She is perfectly charming. You should have introduced us sooner.'

He nodded. Of course he should have. He had attempted it. It had not been his fault that he had failed.

The smile that she was using on him was dazzling, as though she knew how easy it was to beguile him. 'We spoke of you, of course. And of the rest of the family.'

They talked about him. Of course they had.

What other common subject could they have? It was rude to tell him of it. But what had he to fear? Of all the people in the world, he could trust his sister to be kind. And, of course, he could trust Margot.

I do. Two simple words, Fanworth...

He had managed to forgive her that. She had been angry. But he had given her reason to be. If he wished her to forgive him, he could not rage at her over every slight. Last night, he had trusted her with his body and been well rewarded for his faith.

But that had not involved conversation.

Now, her smile looked positively smug. Could he ever truly trust a woman who knew his greatest weakness and mocked it on their wedding day? She might sound sweet, but today that honeyed tongue had put the servants in their place with just a few words. He had admired her ruthlessness. But then, she had been using it on others.

'Fanworth.' She waved a hand in front of him, to gain his attention. 'Stephen.'

It was only then he realised that she had continued speaking and he had not heard a word.

'Excuse me?'

'I asked if you were enjoying the dinner.'

'It is fine,' he assured her.

She gestured to the plates on the table. 'Do you have a favourite, perhaps?' She was trying to persuade him to speak.

He looked down at the dishes set before them. Duck in burnt butter. Pickled beetroot. Potted pigeon. Pears in puff paste.

It was a trap.

His father might use force and shouting to make his point. But his wife was a subtle creature. Now that he had taken her into his life, there were a hundred ways she could find to make him miserable. If there were any weaknesses she had not already guessed, she was likely to learn the rest from his sister. And he had no one to blame but himself. He had been the one to court her, accuse her and seduce her. He had made her his enemy.

He had created his own hell.

He said nothing. To speak was to give her ammunition. Instead, he tossed his napkin on the table and left the room.

Chapter Sixteen

Margot crumpled the note in her hand. She had not seen her husband in days. And now he chose to communicate in writing. It was outside of enough. The worst of it was, she had no idea what she had done to make him angry again.

In her opinion, things had been going quite well. They had proved they were more than compatible, once the lights were out. And after speaking with his sister, some of her reservations about the marriage had been laid to rest. There was still much to discuss, of course. She still did not understand the matter of the necklace.

But to discuss, both parties had to speak. And for some reason, he had gone from speaking little, to not speaking at all. She had no idea what she'd done to cause the change.

She'd returned home early, specifically to please him. They'd dined at the table and she had dressed in a manner befitting the wife of a great man. If he could find nothing good to say about her, the least he could have done was remark on the food. The cook had outdone herself and the quality of her portion had been the equal of his. A single taste of her plate would have proved to him that he would not have to involve himself in domestic strife or the running of the house. She was perfectly capable of managing the staff on her own.

Her efforts to please him had been for naught. He'd stared at her over dinner as if he'd never seen her before. Then, with no warning and not a word of explanation, he had got up from the table and abandoned her.

She had assumed that they would have time later, in bed, to talk. She had even planned to playfully remind him that he was still entitled to one more night of her company. But he had not been in his room when she had gone to bed. Even though she'd arisen early the next day, he was not there. It looked as if he had not come to bed at all.

And so it had gone, for several days. To question the staff about the location of her husband after only a week of marriage would embarrass her in front of servants that had only just come to accept her as mistress. And as it had repeatedly over the last few weeks, she felt the creeping suspicion that he'd got all he wanted from her, and had lost interest.

Now, this. A curt note reminding her of her sister's reception, this evening, and his request that she be dressed and ready to accompany him at eight. Apparently, though they did not speak in private, they were to be a happy newlyweds in the eyes of the world. And he expected her to be the beautiful ornament suitable to a man too proud and well born to have an ordinary wife.

If he meant to escort her in silence, it would be an even greater ordeal than she had expected. Margot had more than enough time to visit with Louisa, since customers continued to avoid the shop. But this morning, the girl had informed her, as gently as possible, that the family would not be attending this evening's festivities. It was quite possible that her visits to the shop would end, as well. Now that the Duke and Duchess of Larchmont were in Bath, they would expect their daughter to stay with them and not with the cousin she had been visiting. Since it had been decided that Larchmont and his lady would not be attending the reception, Louisa had little choice but to remain at home with her needlework.

So, his family was not willing to celebrate the union. If the ledger book told a story, the rest of Bath meant to avoid her as if she had some contagious disease. If no one liked them, then why were they bothering to play-act their happiness? Perhaps she would simply ignore his command and pretend she had forgotten the invitation. She would work later than usual, even if it meant sitting in an empty shop.

Then she remembered Justine, so eager for her happiness that she had orchestrated the wedding, and the party to celebrate it. If the evening was a poorly attended disaster, it would be up to Margot to console her sister, thank her for her efforts and pretend to be happy, just as she planned to do in her marriage. And, if Fanworth wished for nothing more than a beauty, she would give him what he deserved.

* * *

She arrived home even earlier than necessary and ate a hurried supper alone before giving herself over to the ministrations of the maid whom her husband had hired for her. The gown they chose was the green of spring leaves, with a deep hem embroidered with white-and-gold flowers. The maid dressed her hair so that tendrils wound down about her face like so many vines in an overgrown wood. Margot had to admit, the finished look was striking. There was something faintly pagan about it, as though a nymph had been dragged from the woods and forced to marry well.

She smiled at herself in the mirror. If the town gossiped that Fanworth had married beneath him, at least there would be no question as to his reasons. And she had just the jewellery to match it. She directed her maid to get the ebony box from my lord's room.

As the door to the connecting room opened, she could hear him on the other side of the suite, swearing quietly as his valet dressed him. It surprised her that the son of a peer had such a diverse and vulgar vocabulary. But he used it with confidence, for there was not a trace of a stammer as he complained about the tying of his cravat.

The cursing ceased as her maid entered and requested the jewels. There were a few more moments of profound silence. Then Fanworth stood in the doorway, cravat still hanging untied about his neck, shirt open at the throat and the ebony jewellery box in his hands. He was staring at her with the same hungry expression he'd had at the dinner table, before everything had gone wrong.

Perhaps he had only wanted her for her beauty. Then she would desire him for his handsomeness. She was sure that, at this moment, they were both thinking the same thing. If they dismissed the servants, she could go to him, lick once against the bare skin of his throat and they would not leave the house or the bed until morning.

He stepped forward and the spell was broken. When she reached for the jewellery box, he held it just out of her reach. 'Allow me.'

Only two words. But they were the first she'd heard from him in days and they struck right to the heart of her. With a casual flick of his finger, he opened the box, reached into it, and removed the necklace she wanted: a narrow band of gold leaves, set with pavé emeralds. His fingers trailed along her skin, circling her throat as he fastened it.

Why could he not speak to her the way he touched her, as if she were the most precious gift in the world? Now he was affixing the matching drops to her ears, his index finger drawing lightly along the shells before settling on the lobes, sliding the wires into place.

She turned to look into the mirror, if only to distract herself from his touch. Her throat tightened at seeing her work reflected back to her. At last, these pieces would be worn in public, just as she had intended. She would see, first-hand, if they were admired.

Fanworth reached out and took her gloved hand, kissing the knuckles before slipping a bracelet on her wrist. It was the emerald viper he had bought on the first day.

She looked down at it, worried. 'Surely this is too much.'

He shook his head and smiled. 'Eve needs a serpent.'

Did he still think her a temptress? If so, he had been resisting well enough lately. But he was right. The bracelet did go well with the gown. And then she remembered the story. 'Eve was...' Not wearing a gown.

His glance swept her body as though he could see through the silk to the woman beneath. 'Later, you may keep the bracelet on,' he said, smiling again. Then he returned to his room to finish dressing.

While the assembly room was hardly full, it was not the barren wasteland that Margot had feared. The Duchess of Bellston greeted her with a warm kiss upon the cheek and compliments on both her marriage and her appearance. The duke smiled and kissed her hand, then exchanged properly sombre greetings with Fanworth as they took their places in the receiving line.

Though she had been to a few routs with her sister, Margot had never been in such high-born company, much less an honoured guest. Then, she remembered her husband held precedence over all in the room but the duke. She must learn to behave as the duchess did, polite, friendly and confident in her place.

If any guests came with the intent of offering a snub, they were properly subdued by the obvious warm relationship the new marchioness had with Bellston and his duchess. Some even dared to enquire, politely, if the jewellery she was wearing was from her own shop.

She acknowledged that it was so. She had designed it herself. In response, she saw speculative looks on the faces of some of the ladies, as though trying to decide if the social awkwardness of greeting the Marchioness of Fanworth from across a shop counter was greater than their desire to be the first of their friends to own one of her pieces.

Beside her, Fanworth greeted both the ladies and their husbands with a cool smile and as few words as was possible. When compared to his disdain, she looked all the more approachable. And to her surprise, the looks cast at her by some of the ladies in the room changed from suspicion to pity. They seemed to be imagining how difficult life would be, in the presence of such a cold and unfeeling husband.

She had been thinking such a thing herself, only this morning. But then she remembered their wedding. There was a lull in the crowd and she glanced at him now, noting the slight frown that creased his forehead and the way his lips pinched in the tightest possible smile. He was not sure what might escape should he relax and speak freely.

This continual wariness must be as exhausting for him as it was frustrating for her. And it must be very lonely. Without thinking, she reached out and touched his sleeve to remind him that she was still by his side.

He started, looking down at her, as though he had forgotten her presence. Then, ever so slightly, his brow seemed to relax and his smile became less threatening. Perhaps she was more to him than a warm body in his bed. He had chosen her to be his life's companion.

When he had visited her in the shop, he had willingly shared his soul. If he could not manage a few simple hellos at a time like this, there was no way he'd have been so open to her, just to bed her. He had loved her, just as she thought. For this union to succeed, they must find their way back to that place of communion.

The first step would have to be hers. She let her hand remain in the crook of his arm. Let him think that she needed his support, if it was easier for him. Perhaps it was true. But it was equally true that they needed each other.

In response, he moved an inch closer to her. And at the approach of the next gentleman in line, his other hand covered hers. The man in front of them bowed and, though he was a stranger to her, greeted her with an overly familiar smile.

She felt her husband stiffen again, as he made the introduction. 'Lady Fanworth? Lord Arthur Standish.'

She should have recognised him without Stephen's help. Now that she had reason to look for it, the similarity between the men was marked. But the younger brother's good looks were spoiled by the fading blue circles under his eyes and a nose which was still a little swollen.

'How do you do?' she said, offering a hesitant smile.

'Not as well as you, I think,' Lord Arthur said. Unlike her husband's superior smile and distant manners, there was something wolfish about Arthur. She suspected, if he should grin, he would show far too many teeth. Then, as suddenly as he had come, he disappeared into the crowd and they were greeting the next couple.

Once the majority of guests had arrived and the line dissolved, Stephen parted from her with little more than a light touch on her hand and a sympathetic smile. Apparently, she was to be left to her own devices while he did whatever it was a marquess did at such gatherings. If his current behaviour was any indication, they stood disapprovingly against a wall, avoiding other people.

She looked back at him and frowned. Something would have to be done about that. But now was not the time to find a solution. At least he had his brother to talk to. Lord Arthur was beside him, speaking to him as though there was nothing unusual in his behaviour.

It was wrong of her to take such an instant dislike to a person. But there was something about her husband's brother that unnerved her. When he was not at her husband's side, she found herself searching the rest of the room for him, as if she feared the mischief he might create if he was not always in sight. When she could not find him, the raised hairs on the back of her neck told her that he was somewhere nearby, watching her.

Perhaps she was right. After she had not seen him for some time and was almost convinced that he had left the room, he appeared before her wearing the same predatory smile he'd shown at their introduction. 'Lady Fanworth.'

No matter what her feelings, this man was her husband's brother. She had little choice but to respond politely. 'Lord Arthur.'

'It is a shame that it has taken so long for us to meet. We are family, after all.'

'You are Stephen's brother.' It was hardly necessary to state that fact. But somehow, she could not muster a warmer acknowledgement of their connection.

'That I am,' he agreed. But the way he was looking at her was not in the least bit brotherly.

'I must admit, Stephen has excellent eyesight, if dubious taste. You are the most handsome woman here.'

An insult wrapped in a compliment did not warrant a response, so she remained silent.

'It is a shame we have not met before now,' he said. It was an innocent statement, but the ironic glint in his eye said something far different.

'I suspect there is a reason for it,' she said, glancing out over the room and taking a sip of her wine. If he had truly wished to meet her he could have searched her out, just as Louisa had.

Arthur laughed in surprise at her sarcastic response, but he did not leave. 'Perhaps it is because I do not frequent any but the best merchants.'

It was one thing to insult her and quite another to insult the shop. 'Then it is fortunate that I do not need your patronage,' she said.

'Of course you do not,' he agreed. 'You have married well enough that you need no one's help.'

'It was not my plan to do so,' she said.

'Of course not. We have my besotted brother to thank for this union. I told him it was unwise.'

And it appeared he had got a punch in the nose

for his trouble. She glanced across the room at her husband who stood as impassive as a statue against the opposite wall. 'Fanworth has a mind of his own.'

'Would that he was less stubborn. He has over-stepped himself, this time. Larchmont will never accept you.' He looked her up and down again as though the flaw in her character were somehow worn on the outside, for all to see.

'What's done is done,' she said in response. 'He cannot exactly *un*-marry me.'

'I suppose not.' Now he was quite obviously admiring her body. 'If I were married to you, an annulment would be impossible. And I have heard that the lower classes do have a greater appetite for certain things than the milk-and-water misses you find at Almack's.'

When one had customers, one grew used to accepting insults with a smile and not responding to them as they deserved. But Louisa had been right. Lord Arthur Standish deserved to be struck, hard and often. Before she could stop herself, Margot had given him a hard slap to his broken nose.

With a curse that was heard by half the people in the room, Arthur doubled over, cupping his offended proboscis in both hands. All conversation stopped as heads snapped to look in their direction. And then it began again. The crowd swirling like stirred tea as those who had seen informed those who hadn't that the new Marchioness of Fanworth had raised a hand to her husband's brother.

Arthur straightened, glaring at her and mopping at the trickle of blood that dripped from his re-injured nose. 'Pratchet was right. When I sold him the rubies he said you were every bit as stubborn as Stephen. Since neither of you would choose the sensible course, I hope you are both satisfied with the results.'

'Infinitely.' Margot felt the reassuring touch of her husband's hand on her arm. 'So nice to see the family represented, Arthur.' There was a long ironic silence. 'If you will excuse us?' Then, with a gentle tug on her elbow, Stephen led her away.

Catastrophe. Fiasco. Calamity.
When one had the time to think, there were

many words to describe the evening other than disaster. Judging by the way Margot was slumped in the carriage seat opposite him, she had thought of all those and more.

In Stephen's opinion, it could have been far worse. It was fortunate that they'd not met his parents, as he'd expected. If Arthur was any indication, he had been naïve to assume Larchmont capable of good behaviour. More likely, he'd have thought it good sport to humiliate Margot as Arthur had tried to do. While she'd proven capable of handling difficult servants and annoying younger brothers, the duke would not be so easily dispatched.

Her victory tonight had not come without cost. After Arthur had gone home to tend his injury, Stephen had remained by her side, to make it clear to the crowd that his sympathies lay with his wife. But as the evening wore on, she smiled less and spoke hardly at all. It was as if, by marrying her, he'd infected her with his own form of misery.

She had not said a word to him since they'd departed the assembly rooms, staring out the window of the carriage without really seeing the streets they travelled. 'I am sorry,' she said suddenly, not turning her gaze to meet his. 'So very sorry. I never intended… It just happened.' Her hands gave a helpless flutter, then covered her face.

'I understand,' he said.

'Louisa was right.' The words came muffled from between her fingers.

'How?'

'She said you had struck your brother. But that he sometimes deserved to be hit. I did not give it much thought. And then…he began speaking to me…' She shrugged, unable to continue.

'Normally, when we Standishes strike each other, we do so in p-private.' The truth sounded even worse when stated thus.

But she looked up at him, with a surprised smile. What had he said to put such hope on her face? 'You are not angry with me?'

'I am angry with myself,' he admitted. 'I should have kept him away from you.' He reached across the space between them and gave her hand an encouraging squeeze. 'What did he say?'

'I will not tell you,' she answered, with a stubborn shake of her head. 'Or you would likely want to hit him a second time.'

'I will do so anyway, if he annoys you again.' And he would do so, gladly. When he looked at her, he felt a fierce wave of protectiveness. It was as if he had been given a fragile ornament to hold, only to see his brother try to snatch it from his hands and destroy it. Now, he must do whatever it took to teach Arthur that this was not some playroom tussle over a toy.

'Why did you hit him the first time?'

'Eh?' His lady wife was looking down at the hand that held hers, rubbing her thumb along the inside of his wrist. It was a simple touch that probably meant nothing at all to her. But at this gentle friction, he could hardly remember his own name, much less hold a conversation.

'Why did you strike your brother? Louisa said it happened before we were married. She said you would not have him at the wedding. And tonight, there were still bruises.'

Had Arthur lied about the reason, implying he was some sort of bullying brute? He chose an answer that was vague and dismissive. 'He meant to cause trouble between us.'

'It was about the rubies, wasn't it? Tonight, after I slapped him, he admitted he was the one who sold them. I was wrong about you.'

'And I you.' It seemed he took the first deep breath in ages. If she knew this much of the truth, the rest was child's play. He took her other hand and gathered them both to his lips for luck before speaking. 'The day I realised you b-blamed me for the theft, I spoke to P-Puh-Pratchet. He ran off, or he might have explained it all...' He squeezed her hand again. 'It was Arthur, all along. When I showed him the necklace you had made, he'd said you must have stolen the stones. Sold them b-back to me as a joke...' His words were full of embarrassing halts and stumbles. But she did not seem to notice. She was leaning forward, listening patiently, just as she used to.

He kissed her hands again. 'I was angry with you for no reason. I had to marry you. I mean, I wanted to marry you. From the first. B-But now, I had to. Quickly. To make up for what I had done. And you would not speak to me.' He was making a mess of it again. It was what came of speaking without preparation. He was getting ahead of himself.

'And you hit Arthur?' she prompted.

'After P-P-Pratchet. Before the wedding. B-because he deserved it.'

'Why would he do such a horrible thing?' Why indeed? She had done nothing to deserve such elaborate plots against her, other than to sell him a few pieces of jewellery.

So he told her the greatest truth of all. 'Because I loved you. We are…not of the same class. It d-does not matter to me. But Arthur wanted to p-put me off you.' He didn't feel it was necessary to also mention his brother's gambling debts.

'I see.' She glanced around her as though waking from a dream. 'Well that did not turn out as he expected.'

For a moment, Stephen froze, amazed at the lack of anger in her response. Then he pulled her across the carriage to him so that she sat half beside him, and half in his lap. 'No, it d-didn't,' he agreed. 'And I am glad.'

And then he kissed her. Suddenly, things were

exactly how he had imagined they would be, when he had courted her in the jewellery shop. She relaxed and let the kiss happen, responding gently, playfully against his barely open lips.

There was no need for passion, although he certainly felt it, whenever she touched him. But they had a lifetime to indulge it. Instead, they shared the sweet kisses of old friends who had finally become lovers. He wrapped his arms gently around her, wishing that it could be this way for ever.

She started suddenly and pulled away. 'There is something I must say, before...'

Before. So there was to be an after, tonight. That was reason enough to smile. 'What?'

'At the wedding breakfast. I did something unforgivable.'

'Let me decide that,' he said, still holding her close.

'I mocked you,' she whispered. 'There was so much I did not understand. I thought I had been tricked into marrying you. And I was angry. You had already apologised and I had not listened. But no matter about that. I never should have mocked the vows you made to me. Especially since you meant them.' This last was said with a kind of wonder as though she still could not quite believe that what had happened was real.

'I d-did,' he said, annoyed that he could still not quite manage the words. 'I love you.' That was much easier. He must remember to say it often. 'I love you.'

'Then what I did was all the more horrible. I know how hard it can be for you to speak. I swear I will never do it again.'

When he stared at her lips, he quite forgot what it was she was apologising for. 'Forgiven,' he said, using it as an excuse to kiss her again. And again.

'Thank you,' she said with a sigh of relief that made her soft and pliant in his arms. She rubbed her cheek against his, giggling as the stubble scratched her. Had he ever heard a sweeter sound than the laughter of a woman who did not mind his flaws? Then she whispered, 'I dreamed of this. Of you. But I could never have imagined how wonderful it is to be yours for ever.' Then, she leaned forward to kiss him again.

It was what he'd longed to hear, since the first moment he'd seen her. So he settled back into the squabs and kissed his wife in return.

Chapter Seventeen

Could happiness be so simple as this?

Her husband loved her. And she loved him in return. His family objected, just as she had known they would. But as she had told Lord Arthur before slapping him, Stephen had a mind of his own. Efforts to part them had only bound them more tightly together. All that mattered to him was their love.

But had she told him of her feelings? They had said a great many things, while in the carriage. It was the first time they'd really talked in ages. But had she said those three, specific words that had meant so much to her when he'd said them?

They were already at home, in their respective bedrooms as maid and valet helped them out of their evening clothes to prepare for bed. She could hear Stephen's good-natured cursing from the other side of the suite, as he tried to decide if a shave before bed was appropriate.

She smiled as her maid helped her out of the ball gown and into the nightgown that her sister had made for her. Then she called out, loud enough for the whole house to hear, 'Do not bother with a razor. I love you, Lord Fanworth, down to the last whisker.'

There was a moment of silence, followed by a hearty laugh. 'As you wish, Lady Fanworth.'

Margot glanced in the mirror and let out a laugh of her own. 'Are you sure it fits?' she whispered to the maid. 'It is...' The word she was looking for was indecent. The lace yoke was cut so low that her nipples peeped between the gaps in the silk flowers.

The maid nodded, then grinned at her. 'It is very pretty, your ladyship. And I think Lord Fanworth will like it very much.'

Apparently so. He had heard this interchange as well and had manoeuvred himself so he might stare at her through the open doors of the changing room.

His valet was there as well, framed in the doorway. His eyes were fixed rigidly on the floor as he removed my lord's boots.

Before marriage, Margot had managed quite well in two rooms with no maid. How things had changed. It was a shock to admit it, but even with the new door, the situation in Fanworth's house seemed rather cramped. If he wished her to dress as a lady and maintain a shred of modesty in front of the staff, there was no way to share a changing room with her husband and a servant a piece.

A short time later, Stephen dismissed his valet and appeared in the doorway of her room. He was wearing the same dressing gown she had borrowed on their first night together. Despite the sheer gown she was wearing, her skin grew hot at the sight of him.

He glanced at her maid with a raised eyebrow and made a little shooing motion to signify that the girl was dismissed.

'We are not finished combing out my hair,' Margot argued.

'Let me help.' He said it as if there was no greater joy than to wait upon her. Then he took his place behind her dressing table and picked up a silver-handled brush, drawing it slowly through her curls.

Her eyes met his in the reflection of the mirror. In reflex, her nipples tightened with desire.

He noticed and smiled. Then he quickly plaited her hair and offered his hand to lead her to the bed. They had not gone two steps before she had pressed herself against him, demanding and receiving a kiss. The rest of the short journey was a staggering, stumbling laughing tangle of bodies that collapsed as their knees made contact with the mattress. Only then did he part from her long enough to look into her eyes.

'Your maid was right. I like this. Very much.' His fingers danced over the lace yoke of her gown, touching skin through the netting.

'You heard?' she said.

'It was impossible not to. We are rather cramped,' he admitted.

'And I suppose your valet heard as well?' Worse yet, he might have seen her.

Stephen kissed her ear. 'Barker does not see or hear anything I do not wish him to.'

How like an aristocrat, to think that he controlled the senses of his household. 'All the same, I would feel more comfortable if we could seek out larger apartments, so that the poor man will have nothing to ignore.'

Her husband did not answer immediately. He had become distracted with the lace again, trying to taste her breasts through the mesh. When he finally raised his head, they were both quite out of breath. 'Do not worry yourself over it. Summer is half over. We will not be here much longer.'

Suddenly, she was not the least bit distracted by his attentions. 'And where are we likely to go?'

'Where does anyone go? London, for the Season,' he said, taking one of her hands and kissing her arm from fingertips to shoulder, lingering for a moment to toy with the bracelet still twined about her wrist. 'And my home in Derbyshire for autumn and Christmas. The house there has all the room you could want.'

'But my work is here,' she said. She had waited patiently to be of age so that she might return from school and take up the family business. She had no intention to quit it in little more than a year. 'I have a shop to run.'

'We will be shutting that, at the end of summer, when we leave,' he said, as though it was something that had been discussed and agreed upon.

'Will we?' she said.

'It is only common sense,' he responded, completely oblivious to her rising temper.

'Is it?' she said.

'What else would we do?' He was undoing the little pearl buttons at her throat, preparing to remove her gown.

What else would they do? She was not sure she had an answer to that. But she had hoped, when the time came, she would have some part in making the decision. She prepared her argument.

And then, she noticed, for the first time in ages, he had been speaking freely and ignoring the small stammers, just as she did when she listened to him. If she chose to fight him, now of all times, she might lose this closeness, yet again.

He had said they would not leave until the end of summer. That meant she had time to persuade him. And judging by the solid feel of his member pressing against her leg, she had means to persuade him that she had not yet exercised. She reached to his waist and untied the sash of his dressing gown. 'Lord Fanworth?' she said, teasing his lips with hers.

'Lady Fanworth?' he responded, capturing them so he might kiss her.

She pulled away. 'Do you love me?'

'Did I not tell you so?' He seemed surprised that she would ask.

'I wish to hear it again,' she said.

'I would rather show you,' he said, stripping the gown over her head and tossing it to the end of the bed.

She placed her hand lightly on his lips, stopping them before he could kiss her again. 'But first, you must say the words. It is our fourth night together, after all. If you wish me to release you from our agreement...'

He growled. 'By morning, you will beg me to renegotiate.'

'But tonight...' she reminded him. 'Arouse me with words.'

He gave in without further struggle. 'I love you.

I worship you. I adore you.' He paused to kiss his way down her belly. 'Since the first moment I met you, I have been yours to command.'

To test him, she spread her legs and guided his lips to where she most wished to be kissed. And as he promised, he worshipped her. Tomorrow, she would hold him to his promise and command that they keep her business. But tomorrow was a long time away. For the moment, she was lost in the present.

Chapter Eighteen

The next day, Margot glanced around the shop as if she had never seen it before, trying to memorise every last inch of it. She meant to broach the subject of its future tonight, at dinner. But i Stephen was adamant that it was just a brief diversion to be cast aside at the end of summer, she must savour every moment here.

She smiled grimly. Of course, if he though such nonsense, he did not know her as well as he thought. With the servants she had been firm With Arthur she had been violent. But with he dear Lord Fanworth there was a much more plea surable way to work him 'round to seeing thing her way.

She had no intention of closing, now that busi ness was increasing again. After the previous evening's party, she'd had a steady stream of customers interested in seeing the source of the jewels that had been worn by the notorious Marchioness of Fanworth.

To ease their minds about a titled lady in trade, she had retired to the private salon and plied them with tea and cakes, before selling stock and taking orders. By mid-afternoon, she had rough sketches for several custom projects to give to Miss Ross so that the girl might practise carving wax for the moulds. The front counter had sold so many buckles, hairpins and snuffboxes that it had needed restocking twice. It was the most profitable day she'd had all season.

Fanworth would be appalled.

She smiled. It was good that she had not followed her first instinct and flatly refused to obey. After an hour in her gauze-draped bed, he showed no interest in discussing the demise of her life's dream. After a week, it was possible that he would not even remember having suggested it. And after a month, she would convince him that it had been his own idea to relocate permanently to Bath.

Such a complete victory was unlikely. But two

months ago, she'd not have believed that a marquess would fall in love with her. The world was a strange and miraculous place.

There was a sharp clang from the brass bell as another customer entered the shop. 'I wish to speak with Lady Fanworth.' The gentleman at the front counter spoke in a voice so commanding that it carried all the way to the back of the shop. Margot did not need to see him to know that he was used to being obeyed. She got up from the divan, smoothed her skirts and went back to the main room.

But once she had seen him, there could be no doubt as to the identity of the man at the counter. The Duke of Larchmont was an older version of her husband. He had more than a touch of grey at his temples and leaned on an ivory-handled walking stick as he glared down into the cabinet of her best work as though it were nothing but tin and paste.

It would have been a lie to say he looked welcoming. But she doubted that he was as bad as the world seemed to think. After all, everyone had been quite wrong about Stephen. It was proof that she must meet the man before forming an opinion of him.

She suspected Arthur was wrong as well. If the Duke of Larchmont did not mean to accept her as daughter, he would not have troubled himself to come to the shop. He had but to ignore her to make his feelings known. If he had come to make the first move of welcome, she would be sure to give no objection. 'Your Grace.' She swept down into her lowest curtsy, averting her eyes.

'Get up, girl, and let me have a look at you. Do not think you can win my favour by bowing and scraping.' When she raised her head to look at him, he was examining her through a quizzing glass as she might look at a stone with her loupe. She remained still as he walked around her in a slow circle, continuing to treat her as if she were an unfeeling, inanimate object.

When he reached the front of her again, he gave a resigned nod. 'I can see why Fanworth took it into his head to marry you. At least the children will be attractive. It does not matter for a boy. But there is little reason to have a girl, if she is not pretty.'

She bit her tongue to keep from explaining that the gender and appearance of her unborn children were not things that could be planned or predicted. Even if they were, it would not be left to him.

He sighed. 'I suppose it is too much to hope that you have wits.'

'I like to think so, your Grace,' she said, struggling to be polite.

'You have learning? Languages?'

'French, of course,' she said. 'My mother spoke it.'

'Immigrants.' His lip curled. 'And manners. Did she teach you those?'

She tried not to think of the blow she had struck when last trying to prove her worth and gave a polite nod in response.

He nodded back. 'Better to remain silent, as Fanworth does. Especially when you are lying.'

'I assume you are referring to last night's altercation with Lord Arthur,' she said, as calmly as possible. 'He was not behaving as a gentleman.'

'We are discussing your behaviour, not his,' the duke replied.

If he expected her to apologise, he was about to be disappointed. 'If such rudeness is customary from him, next time I will be prepared for it and refuse to acknowledge him, should he speak to me.'

The duke laughed. 'Just as my son does to me. The two of you are very well suited.'

'Thank you,' she said.

'It was not meant as a compliment.' He set his stick across the glass of the counter beside them and leaned forward, glaring into her eyes. 'It is too late to be rid of you, short of bundling you into a sack and throwing you into the river like the mongrel you are. But the least you can do is to refrain from embarrassing the family further than you already have.'

'I have no wish to bring shame upon my husband,' she said. It fell short of allegiance to the Larchmont name, but it was the best she could manage.

'That is more than he can manage for himself,' the duke said, with a sneer. 'And not nearly what is required, if you are to be the future Duchess of Larchmont. I expect you to deport yourself as a lady and not behave like some common trades-woman.'

She hoped that he meant something simple, like being dressed by the right modiste or not slapping members of the immediate family in public. 'I will do my best to behave in a way that honours your name, your Grace. Last night was an aber-ration and it will not be repeated. Give me time and I will prove to you that the manners of a com-mon tradeswoman are no different from those of a well-born lady.'

'I have no desire to learn anything of the man-ners of your class,' he said with the sour frown of someone who has seen something awful in the gutter. 'For as long as there has been a Larch-mont, there has been no such creature in this fam-ily. There will not be one now.'

He put his full weight upon the counter and leaned forward until his face was inches from hers. 'You will close this shop, immediately. Then you will retire to Derbyshire for as long as it takes for your past to be forgotten.'

Was she really so repellent a choice that she must be hidden away from society? Even her husband did not demand such extreme measures when planning for the future. She took a breath, being careful to control her temper. 'I am sorry that our marriage displeases you, your Grace. But I cannot simply close the shop with no notice. There are employees to be provided for, creditors to pay, stock to liquidate... Even if I wished to, it is more complicated than just closing the doors and walking away.'

'I beg to differ.' Without warning, he shifted his weight and pushed down, hard, on the cane resting on the countertop. The glass under it cracked from end to end with a musical clink.

One of the shop girls let out a frightened shriek and Jasper took a step forward, as if fearing he might need to protect her from further violence.

Margot held a hand up to stay him and calm the girl.

The duke ignored them all and picked up the cane. Then, he stared down at the ruined glass. 'This is only my first visit to your little shop. But it is obviously a very dangerous place. There is no telling what might happen to the staff, or the customers, should it remain open. As I said earlier, you must close it immediately.'

She stared down at the glass as well. When she had imagined incurring the displeasure of the peer, she had thought it would be a genteel punishment: a direct cut or a few harsh words. She would never have imagined vandalism and direct, physical threats.

It had been naïve of her to think that anything good would result from this meeting. The Duke of Larchmont punished her husband for an imagined weakness and doted on Arthur, who had not thought twice about sending an innocent woman to the gallows for a theft he'd committed. To find that such a man was warped by pride and the need to control others should not have been a surprise.

And now, he cupped his hand to his ear. 'Perhaps I am going a trifle deaf with age. I did not hear an answer.'

She had not answered, because there was no point in reasoning with a madman. For now, she needed to do what she could to get him from the shop. Then, she needed time to think. Once again, she bit back the things she really wanted to say, and managed, 'I understand, your Grace.'

'See that you do.' With that, he gave a single, sharp tap at the centre of the crack. The ruined glass plate shattered, the shards falling to cover the diamonds on display beneath.

Chapter Nineteen

Something had changed.

After the previous evening, Stephen assumed that almost all the difficulties between them had been sorted. She knew the truth about the rubies. He had been able to speak freely again. They had shared her bed. And that had been after he'd mentioned his plans to take her away at the end of the summer.

He was still awaiting the argument on that subject. He'd win it, of course. There could be no other result. But for such a tiny armful of woman, Margot was surprisingly strong willed. That she had accepted his words without question or contradiction made him suspicious.

But last night, he'd had no desire to question her on her feelings. Talking had been the last thing on her mind as well. And it would have taken more strength than he possessed to resist the new Lady Fanworth when she was dressed in nothing but a thin lace gown and an emerald bracelet.

She was almost as alluring now, seated across the dining table from him in blue silk. The lace and sequins on the bodice drew his eyes to the gentle slope of her breasts, firing his imagination for what might happen when dinner was finished and they had retired for the night.

But there was no sign that she was having similarly pleasant thoughts. She was thinking about something, he was certain. She stared down into her plate with a slight frown, but did not eat.

'Is the food not to your liking?' He had thought the matter settled.

'No,' she said. 'It is delicious.' Then she picked up her fork and began to eat, as though seeking an excuse to avoid conversation.

In an effort to distract her, he questioned her about her day. She answered in monosyllables, if at all. It was a strange inversion of the last weeks, where she had been the one to talk and he had evaded. Now, when at last he was ready and eager to speak with her, she spoke as few words as possible.

Then, he noticed the handkerchief wrapped tightly around one of her fingers. 'What happened there?'

She looked up, startled. 'There was an accident. In the shop. Broken glass. As I was cleaning up, I cut myself.'

Hs stood up and went to her side, taking her hand gently in his and unwrapping the cloth. 'Does it hurt?' It did not appear to be deep, but she looked near to tears.

'It is all right,' she said.

'You work too hard. You must take better care of yourself.' He kissed the finger and wrapped it again.

'I have been thinking that, as well,' she said and took a deep breath. 'In fact, I think you are right about giving up the shop.'

Of all the things likely to come out of her mouth, he had not expected this. 'At the end of summer,' he reminded her, feeling uneasy.

'Or sooner,' she said. 'Tomorrow is Sunday and

we are closed. I do not have to worry for a day or two.'

'You do not have to worry at all,' he assured her. When he had first decided that they must marry, hadn't that been his fondest desire: that she should never have to worry about anything again?

But she did not seem to hear his reassurance. She was staring down into her plate again, poking listlessly at the food with a fork. 'Perhaps, next week, it would be possible to find Mr Pratchet... He wished to own it. I might sell it to him. Or not...' The words were fairly pouring out of her, now that she had begun to speak. But she did not seem any happier for her decision.

'Before we married, you were quite adamant about Mr Pratchet not taking control. This is quite a change of opinion,' he said cautiously.

'I can think of no one else,' she said, setting her fork aside as though she had lost her appetite. 'Justine would not want it. Her memories of the place are quite horrible. When it came fully into our control, she wanted to close it and forget it had ever existed.'

'Women are not meant to run businesses,' he

said, repeating what he had always assumed to be true.

She gave him a tired look, as though she had heard the words too many times before. 'Perhaps not. But there was little choice in the matter, since my father had daughters and not sons.'

He started to speak, and then stopped. Logic dictated that if a business owner had daughters, then the business should fall to the men they married. But that would have meant that she should have married Pratchet, who wanted the business more than the woman, and not a man who wanted her, but had no need of a jewellery shop. Perhaps that was the logical argument. But when it ran contrary to what he had wanted to do he'd had no problems ignoring it. Why should it be any different for her?

'We sisters knew that some day the business would fall to us and we prepared accordingly. We had played in the shop since we were little. And though Mr Montague was a horrible man, he was an excellent jeweller. He taught us everything there was to know about the stones, the metals and the making of jewellery. We learned our letters and our numbers.' She smiled faintly. 'Arithmetic works just the same for a woman as it does for a man. If you were to examine my bookkeeping, you would find it kept in a reasonable hand and totalled properly at the bottom of the ledger.'

Then the smile was gone again. 'But Mr Montague really only wanted the money. And Justine wanted her freedom. I was the only one who really cared about the shop. I planned for years so that I might be ready to take it on. And I have done well. Or, at least, I did. If I cannot have it...'

She spoke of the place as if it were a living thing. And a precious one, at that. It was not just some stray dog that could be put out when it became too inconvenient to keep. By the look on her face, she would be no more willing to abandon a child then she would shutter the windows and lock the doors of de Bryun's.

'Are you quite sure you are ready to leave it?' She had come to the decision on her own, just as he'd wished. Why did it not make him happy?

'You wish me to close it, do you not?'

'Well, yes.' He did. Or, at least, he had. Now, he was not so sure. 'But when we have discussed it before, you have been quite adamant on the need to ensure the livelihoods of your staff.'

'I must see to their safety as well,' she said. It was an odd statement, after the assurances she had given him about the minimal risks involved in her job.

'You promised me before that if you were worried for your safety you would let me protect you,' he reminded her.

Hope flared in her eyes for a moment. Then the look of misery grew deeper, as she became even more obedient. 'Of course. But as you pointed out to me, yesterday, it will be difficult to run the place with the responsibilities I am likely to have as your wife.'

'That is correct.' He thought of his mother and what she did to fill her days. She called on friends in the morning. In the afternoon, she sometimes shopped. She went to dinners in the evening. When they were home, she might visit the sick and the poor. If she stopped doing any of those things, it would not have mattered one whit to the duke, or the people around her. She kept busy. But he would hardly have called what she did 'responsibilities'.

But Margot had pointed out to him on several occasions that she already had them. It was ludicrous to insist that she accept idleness for propriety's sake. 'Perhaps there might be a way to keep it open part of the year. Summering in Bath does not conflict with a London Season.' What was he saying? Hadn't it been his wish that she stop work and devote herself to him? But now that she was considering it, he felt no happier about it than she did.

She shook her head. 'It is better to make a clean break of it. I cannot ask my staff to work half a year, and wait for me to return. It would not be fair.'

'I see.'

'And there is your family to consider,' she said.

'My family?' It was strange that she would think of them, since he spent little enough time considering their feelings. 'If you are thinking of yesterday's meeting with Arthur, put it from your mind.'

'It is not that,' she said. 'I am sure your father would prefer that there not be a shop girl in family.'

'My father?' Stephen laughed. 'My father can

go to hell and take his opinions with him. When he does, I will be Larchmont. And I do not care a fig if my duchess has a shop.'

'You don't?'

'I don't.' Perhaps it was just a contrary wish to do the thing that would most annoy Larchmont. Or perhaps it was that she was smiling at him for the first time all evening.

He put an arm around her shoulders, drawing her out of her chair and away from the table. 'It is plain that talk of closing de Bryun's upsets you. We can discuss it tomorrow. Or some other time.' There were weeks left before the season changed and they must leave for home. 'But we will find a way to handle it that will be satisfactory to all concerned.' He kissed her cheek.

And as they always did, when he was this close to her, troubles did not seem so important. 'All that matters is that we are together.' He kissed her again. 'Although I do not know what I shall do with my nights, now that I have used up all my time with you. Last night was four, was it not?'

This actually coaxed a grin from her. 'Nothing

happened on the second night. I do not think we should count it.'

'On our wedding day, you suggested I save my last visit to your bed for a special occasion. Christmas, perhaps. Or my birthday, which is in March.'

'March is a very long time away,' she said.

'It is,' he agreed.

And quite suddenly, she was in his arms, clinging to him so tightly that it would have taken all his strength to part from her. 'Then let us make the last night last for ever,' she whispered. 'Just promise me, that, no matter what might happen, we will not be parted.'

'Never,' he agreed.

'Then it will be all right,' she said, as he manoeuvred them towards the stairs and bed. 'As long as I have you, the rest does not matter.'

Margot awoke alone the next morning in her husband's heavily curtained bed. Just beyond the velvet, Stephen was assuring his valet that he had no intention of leaving the chamber until evensong, if then. Breakfast should be brought to the room. Tea as well. Nothing else was required from the servants for the rest of the day.

And then the bed curtains parted again and he returned, throwing himself back on to the mattress. 'There. Sorted. I will make the night last for ever, just as you commanded. Come to me, my love.'

She did not need to comply, for the force of his return had bounced her to his side. His arms were about her again and she felt warm and protected. The slight throbbing in her cut finger made her snuggle even closer to him. Perhaps there was madness in his family. Stephen seemed quite normal, as did Louisa. But Arthur and the duke... She shuddered.

'Cold?' He pulled the comforter over them and she did not have to explain. 'Let me take care of everything.'

'That would be nice,' she admitted. Not even the duke could harm her, if she was with Stephen. Though he had wished aloud that she could be thrown into the river, she doubted that he was liable to carry out the threat.

It annoyed her that one visit from the man had

left her ready to give up. But, in her defence, it was one thing to stand up to the likes of Arthur and Mr Pratchet, and quite another to stand alone against the wrath of a peer. Larchmont had almost infinite power and wealth, and he had already taken a dislike to her.

He was also quite mad. The interaction with him had shaken her more than she'd expected. There was something in his eyes that hinted a broken counter was the least of her worries, should she have further dealings with him.

Stephen noticed her mood and made a soft, shushing sound in comfort. 'What is it that troubles you so?'

She should tell him about the visit from the duke. She should have told him immediately after she had returned. But it seemed there was trouble enough between father and son, without her adding to it. 'Nothing, really.' Perhaps, when she had got over the shock of his first visit, she could seek out Larchmont and assure him of their plans to leave Bath. Then she could explain to Stephen that any potential problems with the family had already been settled.

'You are not worrying about the shop again, are you?' He pulled her on top of him. 'Stop it immediately. I have found a solution that will satisfy us both.'

'Really.' It was probably the plan to stay in bed with him until she no longer cared. That solution was impractical, though it had certain advantages.

'You must appoint a manager. What's the fellow with the ears?'

'Ears?' To the best of her knowledge, all men had them. Even the man currently easing her into a more comfortable position on his torso sported a pair.

'The tall chap in the front of the shop, with ginger hair and…' Stephen cupped his hands to the sides of his head and flapped them.

'Jasper,' she said, embarrassed at noticing a resemblance.

'Train him up on the running of the shop, just as you said you are training a girl to do the goldsmithing. You might continue drawing your designs wherever we go, just as other women sketch flowers. Then you might visit Bath periodically to deliver them and be sure that things are running smoothly. We could return in summer, of course.'

Jasper was the only clerk she had retained from the dark days when Mr Montague had run the shop. He knew more about it than anyone, other than herself. There had been only a small amount of disruption on the days she had been late this summer.

And Jasper had been the one to encourage Miss Ross to take over the workbench. Margot might not have come to that decision without his help, since she had been set to advertise. But it appeared that it had been a wise one.

'You are thinking about it, aren't you?' Stephen gave her an encouraging smile.

She nodded and smiled back.

'While I would not normally encourage a woman in this position to think of another man, today I will allow it.'

She glanced down to notice that she was straddling her husband in a way totally inappropriate to be discussing business. 'You are sure you would not find it embarrassing to have your family associated with trade?'

'It is not as if my name is on the door. Nor do I mean to stand in the window hawking watch fobs to a holiday crowd. And I have never been ashamed of you.'

It was true. He had been vexed with her, he had lusted after her and perhaps, for a time, he hated her. But he had never given an indication that she was an embarrassment to him.

And Larchmont was not embarrassed, so much as angry. She would assure him of her plan to distance herself from contact with the customers, and remind him of Justine's relation to Bellston. Her sister still owned half the business and no one remarked on it at all. 'So we might not have to close the shop at all,' she said thoughtfully.

'Not if you do not wish to.'

'I do not,' she said, relieved to be able to speak honestly.

'Very well, then.' Her husband lay back upon the pillows, and placed his hands upon her hips to guide her. 'You may now reward me for my brilliance.'

Chapter Twenty

Margot had married the most brilliant man in England. It was an overstatement, perhaps. But not by very much.

When the shop had opened again on Monday, she had pulled her senior clerk aside and made her proposal to him. His eyes had widened, just as she suspected hers had, when Stephen had made the suggestion to her. It was as though he could suddenly see possibilities that had not occurred to him before. But rather than accepting out of hand, he had requested that they go into the office and discuss things in detail.

As an employer who was used to being promptly obeyed, she had found it annoying. But as a shop owner searching for a competent manager, she had been secretly pleased. He had wanted to negotiate not just a rise in pay, but hiring of additional staff, changes in the scheduling and the implementation of several of his own ideas as to the display of stock. While he might not know the craft as well as she did, it was clear that he understood the running of the business.

The next day, as they had arranged, she arrived several hours later than usual to find Jasper, now called Mr Suggins, wearing a smart black suit and smiling over the counter as he welcomed customers to de Bryun's. The shop was immaculate. The staff was tidy as a paper of pins. The transactions were recorded correctly in the accounting book. There was very little for her to do, other than work with the more exclusive customers and guide Miss Ross in the casting of a hand clasp for a necklace.

Since she did not have to stay late to lock the doors, she was home in time to dine with her husband. After, she climbed into his bed, secure in the knowledge that she did not have to rise from it before the sun was fully up. While she did not precisely enjoy turning the minutiae of business over to another, she could become used to it.

* * *

How things had changed in just a few days. A week had passed and she was enjoying a cup of tea in the private salon, doodling designs for a series of bracelets and actually looking forward to the time that she could go home to Stephen.

Suddenly, her peace was disturbed by the clank of the bell and the crack and bang of the shop door swinging wide on its hinges to strike the frame before slamming shut. While it was inappropriate to scold a customer for carelessness, this one should use more caution, lest he break the window glass.

Broken glass.

There was no need to look into the front of the shop. She knew who had come. And all her plans for their next meeting, to stay rational and pleasant and have a discussion, had fled out the door before it could shut.

He was asking for her again. He sounded reasonable. It was a lie, of course. Reasonable men did not break things to prove a point. Perhaps, if she stayed still, like a rabbit in a thicket, he would not realise that she was here. Maybe he would go again.

Dear, sweet Jasper was lying for her, denying she was in the shop. But it was not working. 'Now see here, your Grace, you cannot simply barge into the back rooms.' It was very brave of Jasper to try to contain the man. If they both survived this, she would thank him.

She could hear the duke's wordless response to opposition: the splintering of breaking glass.

She was up and moving before the last pieces hit the floor. If she wished to prove herself worthy of the Standish name, she must not let him find her hiding in a back room like a coward. When she arrived in the main room, the last of the customers were scurrying out the door and Larchmont's cane was poised and ready to strike the next mirror on the pillar beside him.

'Stop this nonsense immediately, your Grace,' she said. Then followed the demand with a curtsy so that he might not notice her shaking knees.

'Nonsense, Lady Fanworth?' He said her name with scorn, as though doubting that lady was the correct term to use. 'There is nothing nonsensical about my behaviour. It is a result of the surprise I feel to see you still here, after the perfectly reasonable request I made, on my last visit.' He was smiling at her as though nothing was wrong. Even with their limited acquaintance she was sure that the expression did not bode well.

'I discussed the future of de Bryun's with Fanworth,' she said, with more confidence than she felt. 'And we immediately turned over its management to my assistant. I will remain as a silent partner, until we leave Bath in a month.' It was an exaggeration. But she hoped it would do.

'You d-d-discussed it with Fanworth?'

He was laughing at Stephen. She had not liked Larchmont before. In truth, she was terrified of him. But this was the first time she could describe her feelings as hatred. 'Do not talk about my husband in that way,' she said, unable to stop herself.

'He needs his wife to defend him, now?' Larchmont's lip curled in disgust. 'I knew he was a fool. But I did not think him a coward, hiding behind a woman's skirts.'

'Stephen is perfectly capable of defending himself,' she said. Anger was good. She sounded stronger, and thus she felt stronger. She lifted her chin and straightened her spine. 'But if he is not here to do so, I will not stand in silence and listen to you speak ill of him.'

'You have spirit,' Larchmont said in a tone that was almost admiration. 'That is a shame. It would go easier for you if you did not.' Then he lashed out with his cane and broke another mirror as a punishment for it.

She did her best not to flinch as the glass crashed to the floor. 'I understand that you are displeased with Fanworth's choice of a wife. There is no need to destroy the shop to make your point.'

He glanced around him and then said, in a voice silky with menace. 'Apparently, there is. I told you to close the place. And yet, a week later, here we are.'

'I am removing myself from the business,' she said. 'I will be gone from Bath in a month. I will rusticate in Derbyshire. Surely that is what you really want.'

'Do not tell me what I want,' he said, tapping his cane on the floor. 'What I told you to do was to close the doors.'

She glanced past him to Jasper, who turned the

sign in the window to read 'Closed'. It would do no good to anyone should strangers wander in and witness the duke's temper. And they might yet save a pane or two of glass by mollifying him. But, your Grace, as I told you before, it is not so easy as that.'

'"But, your Grace,"' he repeated in a mewling voice. 'Do I need to turn the key in the lock for you?'

'There is more to it,' she said, as patiently as possible. 'There are still orders that need to be filled. And taxes to be paid. I cannot just turn the staff out in the street.'

'Trifles,' he barked, waving his stick wide. 'I gave you a simple instruction. You disobeyed.'

His tone implied that punishment was inevitable. He wished to break things. Most of all, he wished to break her. She could deprive him of that, at least. 'I obey only one man and he is your son. And I do not think Fanworth agrees with your plans for this shop.'

That was all it took to drive Larchmont the rest of the way to madness. The cane came down hard on a glass display table by the door, striking a vase full of flowers so hard that it shattered against the opposite wall. When the cane came up again, i hooked the chiffon curtain, tangled briefly with it before bringing it to the floor.

Jasper gathered the shop girls and herded them from the room, shutting them in the office for their own safety. Then he came back to defend her.

She caught his shoulder before he could attempt to stop Larchmont from further destruction. If he raised a hand against a peer, he would be lucky not to hang.

He wordlessly accepted her caution, but positioned himself in front of her to protect her from flying glass as the cane rose and fell, over and over. They had repaired the front counter since his last visit—now it was ruined again. A back swing hooked the leg of another little side table sending a display of perfume bottles crashing to the ground.

'Enough,' Jasper said, unable to remain silent 'You have made your point, your Grace.'

He glanced at the boy with a raised eye brow

'No more? I do not think she is convinced, as of yet.'

By the time he was sure, she had lost three more mirrors and a second display case. And, as always when one was dealing with a member of the peerage, there was little she could do but watch it happen.

He took a deep breath, as though the exertion had winded him, then smiled and leaned upon his cane again. 'There. I feel much better about the place now. You must shut the doors, if only to clean up the mess. If you open them again, I will return and do just as I have done today.'

'That will not be necessary,' she said. Louisa had been right. It was best just to avoid the man if he was in a bad mood. Her husband avoided him as well, probably because his behaviour was dangerously unpredictable. But no one had told her what to do if the mad peer sought you out.

'I suppose you will go running to your husband over this. If he is smart, he will do nothing, just as he normally does. He has learned to hide from me. I allow it, as long as he keeps his mouth shut in public. But if he crosses me on this, tell him

I shall dog his steps about town, until he reveals himself as the stammering idiot he is. He deserves it, for bringing you into the family.'

She had assumed that if she married above herself, she would meet with some objection. It had not mattered to her until now. What harm could snubs and unkind words do her?

But she had never imagined physical violence. Nor did she want to see her beloved humiliated in public, made to suffer for loving her. This madness had to stop, even if it meant the loss of the one thing that had value to her. 'It will not be necessary to bring Fanworth into this,' she said, grinding her teeth to stop them from chattering. 'From this moment on de Bryun's is no more.'

'Very good,' Larchmont said, smiling over the destruction as if it was an improvement. 'Now that we have settled this matter, we must see if you can persuade me that you are worthy of my name. If not? Further corrections will be necessary.'

She did not hear him go. In truth, she did not hear much of anything for a time. Fear blotted out all other senses. But as her knees gave out and she sank to the floor, her last coherent thoughts were of what he might do to her the next time she failed to live up to his expectations.

Chapter Twenty-One

'Lord Fanworth.' Mrs Sims poked her head into the salon, where Stephen was reading. Her normally placid expression was replaced with worry. 'A girl is here, from the shop. There has been some sort of trouble.'

He set aside his book with a smile. 'What sort of trouble? Has someone lost an earring?' His smile faded, when he saw the girl, a petite brunette, her starched de Bryun's pinafore rumpled and her face stained with tears.

'Tell me all.'

But the girl, Susan, could barely get out a sentence around her tears. 'A madman came into the shop. Everything is broken.'

Stephen seized her arm. 'Lady Fanworth. Was she hurt?'

'I do not think so.'

The girl was useless, if she could not reassure him. 'The carriage. How soon can it be ready, Mrs Sims?' Any delay would be too long. It took him only a moment to decide that the girl should wait for it and guide it back, with the driver and two stout grooms. He would set out on foot.

Without the bother of a vehicle, it took only a few minutes to cross the Circus and run down George Street to Milsom. But when he reached the shop, he found the shades pulled, the sign turned to 'Closed' and the door tightly locked against him.

Damn it to hell. Why had he not asked her for a key? At a moment such as this, he should not have to be left pounding on the doorframe.

The door opened a crack and a girl who he had not seen before whispered, 'We are closed, sir.'

'Not for me.' Had it really been so long since he had been here that the staff did not know him? He forced his boot into the crack in the door before she could shut it again.

'Lord Fanworth.' The ginger with the ears appeared from behind her and opened hurriedly. 'Of course. Come in.'

'Where is my wife?'

'Safe, my lord. But shaken.'

The room was in chaos, the floor littered with broken glass and scattered jewellery. It was silent other than the clank and tinkle of the cleaning in progress and the quiet weeping of one of the younger shop girls. The boy led him through the midst of it, to the private salon where Margot sat on the white-velvet couch, twisting a handkerchief in her hands.

'What has happened here?'

'Nothing,' Margot stared towards the wrecked front room, dry eyed and impassive.

'A robbery?' If that was the case, he should never have allowed this to continue. Or at least he could have posted a man to keep her safe.

She was shaking her head. 'An accident. Nothing more.'

'An accident.' It looked as if a whirlwind had got in through the front door and jumbled the contents of the room.

'Nothing of importance,' she said hurriedly.

'But we will be closing the shop after all. If I must replace all of this…' She swept her hand about the room and gave a light and very false smile. 'It hardly seems worth the bother.'

'Closing?' Had they not just agreed that closing was not necessary? He turned his attention to the new manager, hovering at his wife's side. 'Enough of this. What really happened?'

Jasper, the ginger, wet his lips for a moment, as though weighing the punishment he might get for speaking against the one he was sure to get if he did not. And then, he said, 'His Grace the Duke of Larchmont wishes the shop closed immediately.' He glanced around him. 'He was most adamant.'

'Thank you for your honesty.'

He turned back to his poor, shattered wife and sat down beside her on the soft white velvet of the sofa. 'This was not the first visit, was it?'

She shook her head.

'The night you came home with the cut finger.'

'He cracked the glass of the showcase with his cane.'

'And why did you not tell me, then?'

'I thought you agreed with him,' she said. 'And

then I did not want to make more trouble between the two of you. After what happened when I met your brother…I wanted to do better this time.'

'My father is not like Arthur,' he replied. But she had learned that through bitter experience. 'And you do not need to be better. None of this was your fault.' It was his. He had known what his family was like. He should have protected her.

'I thought our plan for a manager and leaving at the end of the season would be a reasonable compromise. I assumed, when I told him… I was wrong,' she said, looking at the mess around her. 'Perhaps if I had not provoked him…'

How often had he thought that when growing up? It would do no good to explain to her that she provoked him by her very existence, much as Stephen did, himself. 'You did not provoke him. There was nothing you could have done,' he said.

'Perhaps the shop was a mistake, after all. I should have known better. Everyone told me not to take this job upon myself. But I was so sure I could manage. And now, look at it.' Her voice was almost too calm, as though she still did not, could not, truly understand what had just happened.

He remained calm as well. It would not do to frighten her again, while she was still recovering from Larchmont. But inside, his blood boiled at the years of injustice. He had felt as she did now, when faced with his father's random displays of temper. He'd choked on the fear and anger, letting it muzzle him.

No longer.

'It is over,' he agreed. 'You will never be treated this way again. Wait for me here. I will return shortly, with the carriage.'

He strode into the main room, glaring at the frightened clerks. Jasper, the ginger, had opened the cash box and was paying off the staff before releasing them. 'Do not dare!' he barked.

Jasper slammed the box shut and jumped away from it, as though afraid that Larchmont's violence ran in the family.

'Clean up the mess. Find someone to repair the mirrors. We will open tomorrow, as usual. Nothing has changed.' He added a second glare to show that it hadn't. 'And find Lady Fanworth a cup of tea.' Then he unlocked the door and went out into the street.

* * *

When in Bath, the Duke of Larchmont always let the same house in the Royal Crescent. Woe be unto any who dared take it ahead of him. The landlord would gladly put another tenant out into the street to avoid angering the peer. It was just one more example of the duke's disregard for the needs of others and the terror he evoked in those that had to deal with him.

And today it would end.

Stephen rapped once upon the door, then opened it himself, not waiting for the startled servant reaching for the handle on the other side.

'I wish to see Larchmont.' The footman quailed in front of him, clearly used to the tempers of the family.

Without waiting for an escort, Stephen walked down the hall to the small salon and paced in front of the fireplace. It would not do to lose a single drop of the rage he carried.

'What is the meaning of this?' His father stood in the doorway.

'You know damn well,' Stephen said.

'Do not use that language with me, whelp.'

Larchmont hated blasphemy almost as much as stuttering. Stephen grinned. 'I bloody well will. Now, let us discuss your damned visit to my wife.'

His father was smiling. Stephen had come to dread that expression as a warning of disasters to come. 'You do not wish me to become acquainted with my new daughter?'

'Until you can behave like a bloody gentleman and not some drunkard, I forbid you from visiting her.'

There was actually a pause before he could respond to this, as Larchmont tried to decide which made him angrier, the insult or the command. Then, he laughed. 'You? Forbid me? You have no authority over the family, boy. And less than none over me. It is clear you cannot control your tongue, or your wife. Someone must step in and protect our honour.'

'My wife needs no controlling.'

'In my opinion…' his father began to speak, brandishing his cane.

'No one has asked for it, you lick-fingered old fool.' Stephen reached out and snatched the stick from the old man's hand.

There was a moment of absolute silence. And then his father staggered from the loss of the stick. 'How dare you.'

Stephen sneered back at him. 'Do not think to feign weakness where none bloody well exists.'

'I have the gout,' his father shouted back at him.

'Damn your gouty leg to hell and back. You can stand well enough when you are using this to strike people and break things, you miserable bugger.'

The older man watched the stick in his hands as though waiting for the blow that had been years in the making. When it did not come, he smiled again, still thinking he could regain control of the situation. 'I am strong enough to deal with that fishwife you married. And you. You are a full-grown man and still quail before me.'

'Do not confuse silence with fear,' Stephen said.

For a moment, Larchmont himself was silent, as if he had finally recognised the threat right in front of him. Then he said, 'What I did was necessary, for the good of the family—'

'Not my family,' Stephen interrupted.

'Something had to be done,' Larchmont argued.

'The future Duchess of Larchmont cannot be allowed to associate with half the people that come into that place, much less wait upon them like a menial.'

'The only one she cannot associate with is you,' Stephen said, looking at the stick in his hands.

Larchmont watched it as well and smiled. 'Since you do not have the nerve to strike me, I fail to see how you will stop me.'

Stephen twirled the stick in his hand. 'I will damned well tell Bellston that you are as mad as King George. When he hears that you threatened a member of his family...'

'A distant link, at best,' Larchmont argued.

'He is closer to her than to you,' Stephen replied.

'We sit together in Parliament.'

'Because he is forced to,' Stephen said. 'There is not a man in England who would sit with you by choice, you miserable cod.'

Larchmont scoffed. 'I do not need friends.'

'It is better to have them than enemies,' Stephen said. 'And you have one of those, right here in the damned room.'

'You are not allowed to say such things. You are my son.'

'D-D-Did I not speak clearly, you old tyrant?' For once, Stephen enjoyed his stutter. 'I am your enemy. What in bloody hell did you think I would become when you raised a hand against the woman I love?'

'Her useless shop, only,' his father corrected. And for the first time in his life, Stephen felt the man give ground in an argument.

'Her shop is as much a part of her as her head or her heart. Threaten it again and I will walk the streets of Bath in a coronet, selling snuff boxes.'

'It is a blot on the family.'

'Not as sodding big as the mess I will make, if you annoy me,' Stephen said, smiling his father's smile back at him. 'I will introduce Margot to the Regent. Have you seen her? One look, and he won't give a tinker's curse who her father was. She will tell the story of your irrational violence…' Stephen smiled, imagining the scene. 'Prinny's had experience with difficult fathers. He'll bleeding sympathise.'

'You wouldn't dare.'

'Should I go to the tattle sheets instead?' The thought made him grin. He spread his hands in the air to picture the words, 'Mad Larchmont runs amuck in Bath!'

'I am not mad!'

'You cannot prove it by your behaviour, you bum-legged Bedlamite.'

'If you try such a thing, I will…I will…' Without even realising it, Larchmont was searching for the cane Stephen still held.

He held it out towards his father, giving him the barest moment of hope before snatching it back and snapping it over his knee. Then he tossed the pieces in the fireplace. 'Now what will you do? I think you are too old to hit me with your bare hands. But if you wish to try, I will defend myself.' The words were sweet, like honey, and he had no trouble speaking them.

'You would strike an old man?' Suddenly his father was doing his best to look feeble.

'If the only way to get through your thick skull is to crack it,' Stephen said. What he felt was not exactly pity. But it was different from the anger he'd felt so long when thinking of Larchmont.

'Or I will humiliate you, just as you always said I would. You fear for the family reputation? I will happily destroy it, if you force me to.'

'You have done that already, by marrying that… that woman with her infernal shop.'

'If that is all it takes to ruin us, then I fault you for creating such a fragile honour.'

Perhaps he did not have to strike the man. Showing him his faults had caused an expression as shocked as a slap.

It was enough. For now, at least. He bowed. 'And now, your Grace, I must go. Back to Milsom Street. I suspect they still need help with the cleaning up.'

Chapter Twenty-Two

'Must we be here?' Margot stared out over the crowd in the assembly room, who all seemed to be enjoying the last ball of the season more than she was.

Stephen shook his head, smiling. 'What sort of woman are you, to turn up your nose at balls and dancing? It is positively unfeminine. Next you will be telling me you do not like jewellery.'

'You know I will not. I am simply tired. I swear, I have worked harder in the last month than I have all year.'

'Because, as always, you take too much on yourself,' her husband scolded. 'You must trust Mr Suggins to do more. And you may always ask me for help. I will put on an apron and work for you.'

She smiled, remembering Stephen's ineffectual attempts at sweeping the floor on the day that the shop had been destroyed. Until that day, she had not thought a broom a particularly complicated tool. But it was clear that he had never used one in his life. Or perhaps he had only been trying to make her laugh. She kissed him on the cheek. 'It is enough that you paid for the new glass and the curtains.'

'And the painters and woodworkers,' he reminded her.

She shrugged. 'Since so much work needed to be done, I felt it was time for a few changes to the rest.'

'I consider it an investment in our shop,' he said, smiling at her.

'Our shop,' she repeated. At times, she still found his change of heart to be rather amazing. But he had returned from talking with his father that day and informed her that the shop was to remain open with the full support of his family. While she suspected that was an exaggeration, she'd had no further visits from the duke.

'You will rest tomorrow, in the coach to Derbyshire,' he said, kissing her hand. 'I know you are not looking forward to the trip. But I assure you, you will enjoy the place, once we have arrived.'

She smiled and nodded. It was plain from his expression, when he spoke of it, that the pleasure of the summer holiday was wearing thin for him. She must learn to be as supportive of his interests as he was of hers.

'But you say you are tired. Do you wish refreshments?' He gave a shallow bow to indicate that it was his pleasure to serve her.

'It would be nice,' Margot admitted, for the heat from the crush of bodies in the room was oppressive.

'Stand here and wait for me. I shall return in a moment.'

'Or I could accompany you,' she said. The spot he had chosen for her was out of the common path, near a back wall of the assembly room. If she remained there, she would not see a single person of her acquaintance.

'Wait,' he insisted.

'I will be over there, by Louisa.' She pointed

across the room to where her sister-in-law was surrounded by a flock of gentleman eager to procure a last dance before summer ended.

'Later, there will be time to speak to her,' Stephen said. 'For now, you must stay here.' He pushed her even deeper into the shadow of a potted palm.

'Are you trying to hide me from view?' Margot said, hands on hips. 'Because I cannot think of a reason you would wish me to stay here.'

'I am trying to surprise you,' he said with exaggerated impatience. 'And you are making it damned difficult.'

'Then I will hide behind the palm tree, just as you wish, Lord Fanworth,' she said, blowing him a kiss as he walked away.

It took only a moment for her to realise why he had been so particular on her exact location. From the other side of the plant that hid her, a voice called out, 'Larchmont!' It was the Duke of Bellston, greeting the other peer in the room.

Another duke, perhaps, but not an equal. The Bellston title was one generation older than Larchmont's. Despite all the family pride he professed, her husband's father ranked beneath the younger, and far more pleasant, Bellston.

Although she doubted he would make a scene in front of the other peer, as Larchmont approached Margot shrank even further into her concealment. Stephen had sworn that she never need see the man again. He had also assured her, if they did meet, the duke would behave as a gentleman. And that seemed almost as unlikely as her husband using a broom.

'Bellston.' The answering greeting was delivered with the minimum of courtesy. If this was the way Larchmont behaved in public, it explained why her husband was thought rude, when he did not speak.

'So good to see you this evening,' Bellston said, sounding positively gleeful. 'I was just saying to Penny that it has been too long since we've seen you.'

'Yes, dear.' Her Grace, the duchess, was not nearly so convincing a liar as her husband.

In response, Larchmont said nothing.

'I trust the waters have helped with your foot,' Bellston continued.

'There is nothing the matter with my foot,' Larchmont announced.

'Of course not,' soothed Bellston. 'So I assume you carry that handsome stick as an ornament. May I examine it?'

Margot put her hand to her mouth to keep from laughing. It had surprised her when Stephen had made this very specific request for a gift for his father. Then he remarked that the old cane had met with an accident. She suspected the accident was similar to the one that had happened to Arthur's nose.

A moment passed as Larchmont relinquished his cane to the younger man.

'Do not worry,' Bellston drawled. 'I will return it to you, if you feel unsteady. I only wished to see the markings on the head. That is your family crest, set in the mahogany, is it not?'

Larchmont grunted in acknowledgement.

'And a wolf at the head, pewter or silver?'

'Silver, of course,' snapped Larchmont, as if no lesser metal would dare contact his skin.

If he was so sensitive to base metals, it was a good thing he did not know about the lead shot she had hidden at uneven intervals down the length of the wood. Though Stephen had remarked that the old ebony cane handled like a rapier, this new one was fit for nothing more than support. It would prove horribly balanced, should one attempt to wave it about, or strike out with it.

'Are those rubies for the wolf's eyes?' asked the Duchess of Bellston. 'How very clever. They are set inside the mouth as well. The beast looks quite savage, does it not, Adam?'

'Ravenous, my dear,' her husband agreed. 'Tell me Larchmont, where did you purchase such a marvellous stick?'

'It was a gift,' the man admitted, sounding rather like he was going to choke upon this act of kindness.

'From de Bryun's, I suppose,' Bellston said. 'We buy all our jewellery there, because of the family connection.'

'Margot is very talented,' agreed the duchess. 'She has redone the hideous Bellston ring for me so that I almost enjoy wearing it.'

Almost? Margot shrugged. But it was exceptional praise from the duchess who had simple tastes for such a great lady.

The conversation continued in a similar vein, with the younger couple extolling her talent until she was quite embarrassed to be eavesdropping and Larchmont became frustrated enough to leave.

'Did you like your surprise?' Stephen had arrived and was holding a glass of lemonade out to her.

She nodded, taking a sip.

'I doubt if he will ever admit it aloud, but he is quite enamoured of the cane,' Stephen said.

'However can you tell?' He had not said two words about it, just now.

'I have seen the care he takes that the crest is visible, when he walks with it. Family pride, you know.' Stephen looked across the room at the retreating back of his father. 'And now we must go to your next surprise.'

'Two in one night,' she said. Although she was relieved to see that he was leading her in the opposite direction from the one the duke had taken.

They worked their way through the crowd to a

quiet terrace at the back where several invalids in Bath chairs were enjoying the music. Seated amongst them, on a low couch, was a pale woman in her middle years. She was obviously beautiful and just as obviously frail. Around her neck were the rubies that had been the cause of Margot's greatest trouble and her greatest joy as well.

'Mother.' Stephen bowed and then bent forward to kiss the woman on both cheeks. 'May I present my wife?'

Margot swallowed nervously, propelled forward by her husband's hand at the small of her back.

'Come closer, my dear.' The Duchess of Larchmont gestured to her, reaching out to take her hands. 'Let me look at you.'

Margot had known the moment would come when she would meet her husband's mother. Despite his assurances that she was very different from Larchmont, she had not known what to expect. Her plan had been to be friendly and polite. But now, face-to-face with the great lady, the best she could manage was an awed curtsy. 'Your Grace.'

'She is a rare beauty, Stephen, just as you said,'

the duchess announced, pulling Margot forward
to sit on the couch beside her. 'There is no need
to be so formal.'

'I scarce know how else to be,' she whispered,
for a moment shocked into honesty.

'You must treat me as you do your own mother,'
the duchess said firmly.

'I do not have a mother,' she said, and then corrected herself. 'At least, I have not had one since
I was very small.'

'How sad,' said the duchess. Then she smiled.
'But I understand you honour her by continuing
with your family's work.'

Somehow, Margot doubted that the duke described what she had done in quite that way. But
for the duchess, she settled for a simple, 'Thank
you. You are too kind.'

The duchess gave a small nod of her head and
touched the necklace at her throat. 'And I see you
are admiring my rubies.'

'They are magnificent,' Margot agreed.

'I was so glad to hear that Stephen had them
reset for me.'

For a moment, Margot hovered on the edge of

fear. It was rare to see her work after it left the shop. And even stranger to see it in this way.

The duchess touched the necklace again. 'It is strange to lose something so precious and have it returned looking even lovelier. See how clever the work is on the gold. And Stephen has promised me that I shall meet the designer here tonight.'

Her first impulse was to turn and run. But she felt her husband's hand at her back, holding her in place. 'And so you shall, Mother. It is none other than my Margot.'

His mother's eyebrows raised in surprise. 'You?'

She could manage nothing more than a small nod of her head.

'Beautiful and talented,' the duchess said. 'When I heard that Stephen had married a shop girl, I did not think that could be right. But to find a lady with such a rare gift? That is entirely a different matter.'

Margot wanted to correct her. When she took on the shop, it was never with the intent of being anything so grandiose as an artist.

But Stephen was speaking and there was no time. 'Yes. It is. When I first chanced upon her work, I had to know the person that had executed it. You can hardly blame me for losing my head.'

He spoke glibly today, without a sign of the halt that she sometimes heard. But it bothered her to think he would lie so easily and to his own mother.

'She has a special room at the back of the shop where she entertains her more prestigious customers,' he was assuring his mother.

'So it is hardly like going to a common shop then,' his mother agreed. 'It would be more a meeting of equals. So much nicer than tramping down Bond Street with the rest of London.' She glanced at Margot. 'You do have a shop in London, do you not?'

'Only the one in Bath,' she said softly.

'Well, that will not do,' the duchess said, with a frown. 'When you are in London for the Season, you must speak to Stephen about finding a property.'

'What would happen to the shop in Bath?' she said, not wanting to seem ungrateful.

'I suppose then you shall have two shops,' Stephen said, with a smile.

'Two,' she repeated, in wonder.

'And we must convince the Regent to give her a Royal Warrant,' the duchess continued. 'I have but to show him the rubies.'

'And Larchmont's cane,' Stephen added. 'She did that as well. And work for Bellston...'

'Really.' His mother gave an impressed nod. 'Then certainly, she must have a Royal Warrant. You must design a birthday gift for Prinny, my dear. One smile and he will be eating from your hand.'

'And buying your jewellery,' Stephen added.

'Of course,' she said, barely able to whisper. If she was to be a marchioness making jewellery, then why would it not be fit for a prince? Then she looked from her husband to his mother and back again. 'But what if he does not think it proper for a woman to be in trade?'

The duchess smiled at her. 'Then, my dear, we will remind him of Lady Jersey and the Duchess of St Albans. Some of the biggest banks in England are run by women, you know.' She gestured to Margot to lean closer, so that she might whisper in her ear. 'That is the problem with men, my dear. They think so small. But we love them, so what can we do?'

Margot looked to her own dear Stephen and smiled. 'Indeed, your Grace. What can we do but love them?'

* * * * *

MILLS & BOON®

Why shop at millsandboon.co.uk?

Each year, thousands of romance readers find their perfect read at millsandboon.co.uk. That's because we're passionate about bringing you the very best romantic fiction. Here are some of the advantages of shopping at www.millsandboon.co.uk:

* **Get new books first**—you'll be able to buy your favourite books one month before they hit the shops

* **Get exclusive discounts**—you'll also be able to buy our specially created monthly collections, with up to 50% off the RRP

* **Find your favourite authors**—latest news, interviews and new releases for all your favourite authors and series on our website, plus ideas for what to try next

* **Join in**—once you've bought your favourite books, don't forget to register with us to rate, review and join in the discussions

Visit **www.millsandboon.co.uk**
for all this and more today!